RUMBLE™
MOVIE NOVELIZATION

RUMBLE™
MOVIE NOVELIZATION

Adapted by **Michael Anthony Steele**

Simon Spotlight

New York London Toronto Sydney New Delhi

SIMON SPOTLIGHT
An imprint of Simon & Schuster Children's Publishing Division
1230 Avenue of the Americas, New York, New York 10020
This Simon Spotlight paperback edition January 2022
SIMON SPOTLIGHT and colophon are registered trademarks of Simon & Schuster, Inc.
For information about special discounts for bulk purchases, please contact Simon & Schuster
Special Sales at 1-866-506-1949 or business@simonandschuster.com.
Manufactured in the United States of America 1221 OFF
10 9 8 7 6 5 4 3 2 1
ISBN 978-1-5344-7661-5 (pbk)
ISBN 978-1-5344-7662-2 (ebook)

1

TENTACULAR TAKEDOWN

Winnie Coyle's heart pounded with excitement as she made her way down the crowded street. And just like the blood pumping through her veins, the townspeople of Stoker flowed through the streets, eagerly moving toward the heart of their city, the Jimbo Coyle Stadium.

"Hey, Fred!" Winnie said as she moved past the diner.

The burly man wiped his hands on his short apron. He looked up and smiled. "Hey, Winnie!"

Winnie pointed over his head. "The new tentacle sign looks good!"

"Thanks!" Fred replied, proudly gazing back at the neon tentacle stretching across the roof of the diner. The tentacle's tip curled around the handle of a neon coffee cup. "It's for Tentacular," he added. "Pretty clever, huh?"

Winnie giggled. "I love it!"

Fred pumped a fist in the air. "Stoker! Stoker! Stoker!"

Winnie joined him in the chant before moving back into the flow of foot traffic. "See you up there, Fred!"

"I hope we win!" he shouted before flipping over his OPEN sign to reveal the other side. It read: GONE WRESTLIN'! WHY AREN'T YOU?

The entire town was excited too. It had been nine long years since Stoker hosted an official World Monster Wrestling match as big as this one. It was a Big Belt night—a fight for the championship!

Winnie bopped along cheerfully, her pink hair, pulled up in two buns, bouncing as she walked. Although she was only sixteen, she knew everything there was to know about monster wrestling. And she was confident that Stoker's new monster had what it takes to be champion. Tentacular was going to win; she just knew it!

Of course, it didn't take a monster wrestling wiz

like Winnie to have confidence in Tentacular. As she neared the stadium, ten shirtless boys marched past her, each with a letter of the monster's name painted on his stomach.

"Ten-tac-u-lar!" they chanted. "Ten-tac-u-lar!"

Just ahead, the stadium loomed before her. The river of fans flowed between towering granite columns and streamed toward the gleaming arched entrance. However, each of them slowed to touch the foot of a bronze statue as they entered. The statue was of a man reaching triumphantly toward the sky. It was Winnie's father, Jimbo Coyle.

Winnie paused by the figure and placed a hand on its right foot. The statue's foot was warm and shined brightly, polished by the hundreds of fans before her.

"Bring us luck today, Dad," Winnie said, gazing up at the statue.

Winnie pushed through the turnstile and ran through the stadium's large entryway. Most of the fans headed toward their seats, but a long line of them stretched toward the gift shop.

"Hey, Winnie!" someone shouted. She spun around to see Hoppy, the hot dog vendor, gliding by. "Pineapple-slaw dog with extra ketchup coming at ya!" he shouted as he tossed a wrapped hot dog her way.

"Yes!" Winnie said as she caught the foil-wrapped snack with one hand. "Thank you, Hoppy."

She marched by the line of waiting customers and past the Jimbo Coyle Museum. It was a large alcove displaying a collection of her father's monster wrestling memorabilia, including his yellow and white hoverbike. Framed photographs showed her father riding the bike, hovering near the head of Stoker's former championship monster—Rayburn Sr. The orange, striped monster had two sharp horns, a long, whiplike tail, and a body rippling with muscles.

When Winnie reached the gift shop, she spotted a woman with short brown hair behind the register. The lady coolly checked out customers as they madly purchased Tentacular bobbleheads, T-shirts, mugs, posters, and every kind of product big enough to sport the monster's grinning face.

"Heads up, Mom!" Winnie shouted as she tossed the hot dog at the woman behind the counter.

Her mother, Maggie Coyle, didn't skip a beat as

she caught the hot dog with one hand, her other hand still working the cash register. "Thanks, Win," she replied. "I haven't eaten all day."

Winnie waved as she walked away. "See you in a bit!"

After a couple of turns, she entered the stadium and made her way down the steps toward her seat. Fred was already there, cheering along with the rest of the town.

Music thumped through the stadium speakers, while giant shafts of light crisscrossed in the night sky. Other spotlights washed over the enormous wrestling ring in the center of the arena.

The circle of giant view screens suspended above the ring sprang to life as the announcer's voice boomed through the speakers. "World Monster Wrestling presents the Smackdown in Stoker!"

On the screens, the WMW logo was replaced with a closeup of the ringside commentator, a goateed man in a sharp blue suit. "Live from Stoker on Avon," said the man. "I'm Marc Remy, welcoming you at home to the biggest night of monster wrestling in years. Right here in the house that Rayburn and Jimbo built."

The camera widened to show a huge monster sitting behind the desk next to Marc. He was green with orange spots, with a small glowing orb dangling from a stalk on top of his head.

"And I'm Lights Out McGinty," the monster said, his oversize mouth stretching into a wide grin. "And I could not be more excited." McGinty pounded the desk, making Marc fly up from his seat. "But with that excitement comes some sadness, Marc. I can't believe it's been nine years since we tragically lost Rayburn and Jimbo."

"Nobody was greater," Marc agreed. "We all miss them."

Winnie felt a lump form in the back of her throat at the mention of her father's name. She glanced up at the huge banners hanging from the stadium's upper level. One showed a closeup of Rayburn; the other showed her father. Her lower lip began to tremble. She missed him so much. But then her chest swelled with pride when she realized that she wasn't the only one.

"Jimbo! Rayburn!" the crowd chanted. "Jimbo! Rayburn!"

"Listen to this crowd," Marc said. "Boy, this is special!"

"But now we are moments away from seeing if Tentacular can bring the glory days back to Stoker," added McGinty.

Suddenly the stadium darkened. The spotlights died, and the music faded. Even the audience grew silent.

"Welcome, monster wrestling fans from every corner of the globe," thundered the announcer's voice. "Tonight we wrestle for the Big Belt."

Suddenly the entire stadium shook as something thudded in a slow rhythm. The noise grew louder and the ground vibrated harder as something huge stepped closer and closer.

Winnie craned her neck to see an enormous figure approach through the contestant entryway. Smoke poured out of the opening, and a laser show danced across electronic panels so only the creature's silhouette could be seen. The monster had beefy arms, broad shoulders, and a shark fin atop his head.

"And now," said the announcer. "From Stoker on Avon . . . the hometown hero . . . the challenger . . ."

It seemed as if the entire audience held their breath along with Winnie.

"Tennnnnn–tacular!" shouted the announcer.

"Yeah!" Tentacular shouted as a spotlight lit him up. He spread his arms wide, splitting them into three blue tentacles on each side. "Come get some of this!" he yelled as pyrotechnics exploded around him. Fireworks blasted into the sky as columns of flames, smoke, and sparks erupted on all sides.

The audience cheered as the immense monster strutted toward the ring.

"The pride of Stoker is in the house," said Lights Out McGinty. "He is ready! Look at him go!"

"Wooo!" Winnie shouted. "Do it for Stoker, T!"

"Ah, just listen to that passion!" added Marc.

"Yeah! Tentacular!" shouted a pudgy man a few rows in front of Winnie. He ripped off his shirt and pointed to his chest. "I've got your whole life story tattooed on my body!"

Tentacular looked down and grinned at the man. His rows of sharp shark teeth seemed to go on forever. "I hope you saved room for the win I'm going to have tonight!" the monster said.

When Tentacular got to the ring, he reached up and wrapped his tentacles around the top rope. Then he hoisted himself into the air, spinning in a perfect pirouette as he sailed over the ropes. When he hit the mat, the stadium lights went completely dark.

"Let's light 'em up!" the monster shouted as his entire body glowed with bioluminescent spots. The roar from the crowd was deafening as the glowing beast struck several poses.

When the stadium lights came on again, Tentacular glanced up and saw the blimp hovering above the stadium. A closeup of the monster's face played on the blimp's video screen.

Tentacular stretched a tentacle around the blimp and pulled it closer. "Who wants a selfie?" the monster asked, posing for the camera on the blimp. "I do! I'm so pretty!"

"Look at those muscles," said Lights Out McGinty. "The guy's traps are busting out of his neck."

"Yeah, T!" Winnie shouted. "Pop! Those! Pecs!" she chanted along with the rest of the crowd. "Pop! Those! Pecs!"

Tentacular released the blimp and struck another bodybuilder's pose. "Here I am!" he shouted as his chest muscles danced up and down, delighting the crowd.

Just then the lights went down again. This time,

instead of Tentacular's light show being the center of attention, the air was filled with the sound of trumpets. The royal fanfare played as spotlights appeared on the opposite contestant entrance.

"And now, here comes the King," boomed the announcer. "Sixty-two feet of pure pain! The Slimy Limey, the No-Bull British Bulldog . . . Kiiiiiiiing Gorge!"

A giant bulldog stepped out into the light and sauntered toward the ring. King Gorge had broad shoulders and sharp horns that would look more at home on a giant steer. He wore a small crown and a flowing royal cape as he looked down his nose at the crowd.

The audience met him with a barrage of taunts and *boo*s.

"Boo!" Winnie joined in.

"Bad dog!" Fred added. "Bad dog!"

King Gorge sneered and waved a dismissive paw toward the audience. "Bow to your king," he said.

"You're going down, Gorge!" Winnie shouted up at him.

King Gorge climbed into the ring and removed his crown and cape. He raised his stocky arms and gazed out at the jeering crowd. The monster grabbed the top rope and roared. Streams of slobber covered the first two rows, better known as the *slime zone*.

"Ladies and gentlemen and monsters," boomed the announcer's voice. "Let's get ready to rumblllllllle!"

"I'm so ready to rumble!" Winnie's mother said as she edged toward her seat. She held an armload of Tentacular stress balls. "Who needs a stress ball?" she asked the surrounding fans. She passed a few out before sitting down next to Winnie.

Winnie hardly noticed her mother arrive. Instead, she leaned forward in her seat, concentrating on the two fighters.

DING!

The bell rang, and the monsters faced off, snarling as they slowly circled each other.

"And this championship match is officially under way," said Marc.

Suddenly Tentacular charged and swung at King Gorge with a splay of long tentacles. The giant bulldog easily ducked beneath the blow, coming up behind Tentacular. King Gorge reached a beefy arm around Tentacular's neck, putting him in a headlock. Tentacular's eyes bulged as the Slimy Limey squeezed.

"This is awesome! Spectacular! Electrifying!" said Marc. "Whatever word you want to come up with!"

Fred hid his eyes behind a tub of popcorn. "Okay. Breathe, Fred," he told himself. "Breathe . . ."

As Tentacular escaped the hold, Winnie squinted her eyes, concentrating on each monster's classic wrestling moves. "Ooh, there it is! The Inverted Cloverleaf! That was Andre's move." Keeping her eyes on the ring, she nudged Fred with her elbow. "He might have this, Fred!"

"Come on. I'm not watching," Fred replied, nervously peeking out from behind his popcorn. "I'm watching, but I'm not watching."

King Gorge jabbed at the side of Tentacular's neck, and Winnie sprang to her feet. "Oh, come on, Ref. That's a gill-gouge!"

All through the first round, Winnie's eyes darted back and forth from the ring to the giant video screen above it. Staring at the ring, she could iden- tify each and every classic monster wrestling move, which she had memorized long ago. On the video screen, she watched close-ups of the monster's faces. Unfortunately, Tentacular's face showed worry and concern, while King Gorge oozed confidence and a general smugness.

"Tentacular came into this match the hot favorite," said McGinty. "But this wily old champ has other ideas."

As the second round began, Tentacular continued to take a beating. Even though he had the reach, King Gorge had the experience. Every time Tentacular would get his tentacles around the bulldog, Gorge confidently licked his nose before whipping the younger monster to the matt.

Winnie shook her head. "Gorge is doing the Irish whip into the flying left hook lariat every time." She cupped her hands around her mouth. "Come on, T!" she shouted. "Watch that elbow smash!"

Tentacular didn't. Winnie cringed and the crowd moaned as the blue monster took an elbow to the face. Fred ducked back behind his popcorn.

Winnie cocked her head. There was something about King Gorge's fighting style that stuck out to her. She recognized all the classic monster wrestling moves; there was nothing new there. No, there was something else that she couldn't quite place.

Once again, Tentacular wrapped his long tentacles around the giant bulldog. He squared his feet and raised his tail, preparing to flip his opponent. And, once again, King Gorge smugly licked his nose before twisting out of Tentacular's grasp. He snatched up the younger monster and slammed him to the mat.

Winnie sprang back to her feet. "Did you see that?" she asked. "He licked his nose again! You saw it, right? Just before he hooks left!"

She studied Gorge's face on the large video screen. She watched as the bulldog licked his nose immediately before slamming a fist into Tentacular's jaw.

Winnie pointed at the screen. "There! He did it again!"

"Did what!?" Fred asked, peeking around his popcorn. "I'm not watching!"

Winnie shook her head and smiled. "It's so obvious." King Gorge had a tell—a small unconscious gesture that signaled he was about to strike. The giant bulldog licked his nose before every attack.

Winnie climbed over the people seated in front of her. "Whoops," she said. "Heads up."

"Where are you going?" Fred asked.

Winnie didn't answer. She scrambled over another row of fans before making it to the aisle. She sprinted down the stairs, accidentally spilling drinks and popcorn.

"Oops, sorry," she shouted back at them, but she didn't slow down. She had to make it to the ring.

Winnie didn't even stop when the stairs ahead of her were blocked by cheering fans. Instead, she jumped to the side and slid down the long metal railing. "Coming through!"

As Winnie slid, she glanced up at the action in the ring. Things still looked bad for Tentacular. No matter what the tentacled monster did, King Gorge gained the upper hand.

"Oh!" Marc Remy shouted. "Gorge has got him in the chicken-wing-over-the-shoulder-drop-face!"

"Tentacular is in real trouble early in this match," McGinty added. "I'm going to go out on a limb here and say that we're in for another coronation of King Gorge."

Winnie reached the bottom of the railing and

kicked off. She flew over more audience members before latching on to a cotton candy vendor's tall pole. Bags of spun sugar flew everywhere as Winnie rode the pole down over the rest of the crowd. Her feet hit the field, and she darted toward the giant wrestling ring. She just reached Tentacular's corner when the bell ended the second round.

"There goes that round!" Marc Remy announced.

Winnie climbed the tall turnbuckle in Tentacular's corner. She scaled the metal struts and reached the top as Tentacular returned to his corner. Now that she was level with the monster's head, she could see how woozy and winded he was. He was almost as out of breath as she was.

Tentacular's coach, Siggy, zipped up on his hover-bike. He hovered just beside the monster's haggard face. "What are you doing?" the short, older man asked. "This is your chance! Focus, T. Remember the game plan? Get him up on his hind legs, then wrap him up with your tentacles."

Still doubled over, catching her breath, Winnie raised a hand. "Wait . . . a second."

"What!?" Siggy jumped in surprise. "Winnie?"

"Wait," Winnie repeated between gasps. "He's

got . . ." She took one more breath. "He's got a tell!"

Siggy scowled. "How many times do I have to tell you, ringside's no place for no little girl."

"He licks his nose every time," Winnie finally got out.

"What are you talking about?" asked the coach.

She pointed across the enormous ring. "He licks before he strikes."

Tentacular dabbed at his forehead with a giant towel. "Is Winnie right, Sig?"

All three of them turned to King Gorge. The humongous bulldog casually sipped from a water bottle while his coach scratched behind one of his ears with both hands.

"You're a good boy, aren't ya?" asked the coach. "Yes you are. Who's a good boy, then?" One of the monster's stubby hind legs kicked as the coach scratched.

Tentacular turned back to Winnie and Siggy. A wide, shark-toothed grin stretched across his face.

Siggy smiled at him and nodded. "Pull up your socks and take this guy out."

Tentacular tossed away the towel and gave

Winnie a wink. "Good call, Winnie. Thanks!"

The bell rang, and both wrestlers moved toward the center of the ring. Now Winnie had the best seat in the house as the two monsters circled each other, looking for an opening.

Then, just as she predicted, King Gorge licked his nose and lunged for Tentacular with lightning speed. This time Tentacular was ready. He dodged the attack and spread his tentacles wide. He grabbed King Gorge by the horns and jerked him off his feet. He swung the bulldog around twice before flinging him into the air.

"Yes!" Winnie shouted.

The stadium erupted in cheers as Tentacular caught King Gorge and raised him over his head. Tentacular let out a deafening roar.

"Yeah, T!" Winnie yelled. "Finish him!"

Tentacular slammed King Gorge to the mat. The vibration nearly shook Winnie off the top of the turnbuckle. The giant horned bulldog didn't get up; he was out cold.

Tentacular roared in triumph as the referee raced in for the count. ". . . eight, nine, ten," the referee finished. "He's out!"

"We did it!" Winnie shouted as the stadium erupted in cheers.

"Oh, yeah, Stoker!" Tentacular shouted as he proudly hoisted the championship belt high above his head. "I'm going to an unnamed theme park!"

Winnie continued to enjoy her special seating as a large crane extended into the ring. Marc Remy stood in its basket as it pushed in toward Tentacular.

"T!" shouted Marc. "Get over here, big guy! You did it. You are the champion. You got the job done. Can you tell us what this means to you?" He stretched out of the basket, pointing his microphone toward the giant monster's mouth.

"Marc, let me tell you," the monster said, leaning forward. "This means so much to Tentacular! But first, I have to thank Stoker."

"I love you, Tentacular!" yelled a fan.

The monster aimed a tentacle at the fan and winked. "Ooh, this town," he continued. "You have given Tentacular everything Tentacular needed to realize Tentacular's dream." He kissed another tentacle and pointed at the crowd. "I love you, Stoker!"

"Awwww!" Winnie said, right along with the rest of the crowd.

Tentacular nodded. "So thank you, Stoker. You will always have a special place in my heart as the place that Tentacular left to go somewhere"—a grin stretched across his face—"much, much better."

"What?" asked Winnie, her jaw dropping with disbelief. The entire audience gasped as one.

"Are you serious?" asked Marc. "You're leaving Stoker?"

"Of course, Marc," Tentacular replied with a shrug. "I'm about to make history, my own history. Can't do that in Stoker. Too much history here already." He pointed a tentacle at the giant Jimbo and Rayburn banners hanging from the stadium roof. "That's why I'm taking my talents to Slitherpoole!"

Winnie dropped to her knees. "No!"

Tentacular motioned to someone outside the ring. "Jimothy, come here!" A young man on a hoverbike floated toward the ring. Tentacular nodded at the man. "This is my ticket to bigger and brighter things, Marc."

The man had a thin beard and was dressed from head to toe in Slitherpoole gear. He held up a finger on one hand while he tapped on his phone with the other. "Let me finish this killer . . . tweet," Jimothy said.

When he was done, he flew down and snatched the microphone from Marc's hand. "That is right, Marc," he said. "Now the big guy can actually win somewhere that really matters." He raised a triumphant hand. "I'm talking about Slitherpoole!"

The audience booed and yelled as Jimothy hovered back up to Tentacular. One of the monster's tentacles took the tiny microphone and held it close to his mouth.

"So thank you again, Stoker," Tentacular shouted above the *boo*s. "Much love! T out!" The monster released the microphone, letting it drop several stories to the mat below.

Winnie fell back, plopping down atop the turnbuckle. She watched in shock as Tentacular vaulted over the ropes and swaggered toward the locker rooms. He passed under an electronic sign flashing: HOME OF RAYBURN AND JIMBO. The monster balled up his tentacles and smashed the sign as he strolled beneath it. He disappeared down the corridor amid a shower of sparks.

2
A TOWN WITHOUT A MONSTER

The next morning, Winnie and her mom sat in the back of Fred's diner while many Stoker towns-people milled around discussing what had happened. Winnie strained to hear what people were saying over the sounds of breaking glass coming from outside. Fred was up on the roof smashing his new Tentacular sign. "Why did I buy this stupid sign!?" he shouted between blows.

Stoker was a wrestling town, and it had invested everything into Tentacular. Winnie couldn't believe all that hard work had been for nothing. She leaned her head on her mother's shoulder. "Mom, what's going to happen?"

"I don't know, hon," her mother replied, putting

an arm around her daughter. "But we've been through worse."

Fred marched through the front door with a baseball bat resting on his shoulder. He was sweaty. "You wanted neon," he said to himself sarcastically. "I said sure, money's no object!"

Jane, the hairstylist, pointed out the window to the tentacle-covered shop across the street. "Have you seen my hair salon?"

Everyone rounded on Stoker's mayor. "What are we supposed to do?" a man asked. "What's going to happen to us?" asked a woman. "The town is nothing without Tentacular," said another man.

The mayor straightened his pastel sports coat and raised his hands, silencing the anxious crowd. "All right, everybody, now settle down," he said. When the shouts of concern fizzled to a small murmur, he lowered his hands. "Look, I know you're all worried. After all, each of us owns a piece of Stoker Stadium." The townspeople glanced at one another, nodding in agreement. "But what you don't realize," the mayor continued, "is that things are actually . . . much, much worse than you know!"

"Hang on, what!?" asked Jane.

The mayor pointed to a woman standing beside him. "Uh . . . our treasurer can explain everything," he said, before lowering his voice. "It's probably her fault anyway."

The woman shook her head as she brought in a large easel holding a giant pad of paper. "Wow, thank you so much, Mr. Mayor." She uncapped a marker as she spoke under her breath. "Pretty sure it's your fault though."

The treasurer drew three crude drawings on the oversize pad. One sketch was of a monster, another was a stadium, and the third was a dollar sign.

"Okay. Let me make it simple," said the treasurer. "Very simple. The stadium cost lots of *money*, okay?" She circled the dollar sign before crossing out the monster drawing. "No *monster* means no *money*." She scratched over the dollar sign before finally crossing out the stadium. "No *money* means no *stadium*, which is *bad* for Stoker." She actually wrote out B-A-D under all the drawings.

Everyone in the diner stared back at her blankly.

The treasurer shook her head in disbelief. "Remember when Pittsmore lost LeBrontasaurus?"

Everyone gasped. "Not Pittsmore!" they said in unison.

"That's right," said the treasurer. "All they have left is that illegal monster wrestling club in that abandoned bobblehead factory."

"Okay. Hold on, everybody," the mayor said, stepping forward. "I'm here to tell you that there is a solution! Jimothy, the owner of the Slitherpoole franchise"—he waited for most of the people to stop booing before he continued—"has offered a lot of money to buy the stadium!"

Everyone's boos turned to cheers.

"That's right," agreed the treasurer. "A *lot* of money."

The diner was filled with hope once again. Winnie and her mother exchanged optimistic smiles while the people discussed the news.

"Thank goodness," said a woman. "We're saved," added another. "Jimothy will get us a monster!" a man declared. "That's great!" exclaimed another.

"Yes," agreed the mayor. "Yes, that is great." He spread his arms wide. "He's going to blow up the stadium and turn it into a parking lot."

The people glanced around in confusion. "A what?" a man asked. "A parking lot!?" asked a woman.

Winnie ran to the front of the crowd. "No! You can't do that to the Jimbo Coyle Stadium!" She shook her head. "That's . . . no!"

The diner was stone silent.

The treasurer simply shrugged. "Sorry, but the whole town will go bankrupt in ninety days unless we sell to Jimothy."

Winnie threw up her hands. "Without monster wrestling we're going to go bankrupt anyway, just later on."

"Exactly!" agreed the treasurer. "Because later is better."

"So, that's it!?" Winnie asked. She rounded on the townspeople. "You're ready to lose my father's stadium? After everything he did for this town?"

"Winnie, look, I'm sorry," said the mayor. "But if you believe we can replace Tentacular in ninety days . . ." He shook his head. "That's crazy!"

Winnie shook her head. "No, it's not. We're a monster wrestling town, and we've got the best coach in the league! Siggy!"

Winnie stormed out of the diner and marched across town. She didn't cool down during the long walk. If anything, she became even more furious at the townspeople for giving up so easily. She also grew more determined to save the stadium with every step. She was full of hope and conviction when she knocked on Siggy's door. However, her confidence was deflated when Siggy told her his news.

"You're leaving, too!?" Winnie asked.

The short coach cleaned out his kitchen cabinets, placing pots and pans into one of many cardboard boxes scattered about. "I'm sorry your feelings are hurt, kid," Siggy said. "But this is wrestling." He shrugged. "It's all about hurt."

Siggy pulled an old blender out of a cabinet. "Hey, you want this blender?" he asked as he pushed it into her arms. "It doesn't have a top, but it still works."

"This town needs a monster, Sig," Winnie pleaded, ignoring the gift. "And with you as coach, we can get a new one! I know we can!"

"I have a monster—Tentacular—and I go where he goes," Siggy said. "That's just how it is, how it was, and how it's always going to be."

"But what about Stoker?" asked Winnie.

"That ain't my problem," Siggy replied. "And

it ain't your problem either." He waved her away. "Go live your life. Go do what you young kids do, whatever that is."

Winnie felt as if she had swallowed a bowling ball. Without a championship coach, what monster would want to come to her town? Winnie couldn't believe she had misjudged the man so badly. He wasn't the man she once knew.

Siggy opened a drawer and pulled out a black plastic disk. "Oh, would you look at that.... I found the lid!" He chuckled as he snatched the blender out of her arms. "Give me back the blender."

3
THE PERFECT MONSTER

Winnie wandered through the streets of Stoker. Even though the bad news was literally hours old, the town already felt as if it was on the decline. Some stores were closed early, while other business owners worked to strip away any mention of Tentacular from their storefronts. Even though they had ninety days to sell the stadium, it felt as if everyone had already given up.

Winnie ambled through town until she found herself walking toward the stadium itself. She hadn't planned on going there, yet she ended up there just the same. It truly was the heart of Stoker.

Winnie stopped at the statue of her father and placed a hand on his foot. Unlike the day before, the metal felt cold, as if all the luck had left along with Tentacular and Siggy. She gazed up at the statue, looking for some kind of guidance. Of course, the statue was silent, offering no help whatsoever. Winnie wished her father were still alive. He would be able to bring another monster to Stoker. He was the greatest coach of all time. And if she were only half the coach he was, she could do it too.

Winnie smiled as she remembered riding on her father's shoulders while he trained Rayburn.

Her father had held up a worn book and grinned up at her. "It doesn't matter how big or strong Rayburn is," her father had told her. "He's going to win because of this." He gave the book a shake. "We train hard, we study our opponents, but most of all, we stick to the game plan."

Winnie's eyes fell on the small book in the statue's hand. It was a representation of her father's playbook. He had carried that book with him everywhere he went. It contained all the best wrestling moves and strategies, along with notes from every match he ever coached. It was everything her father knew about wrestling, all in one place.

Winnie gave a knowing nod. Perhaps the statue

had given her some guidance after all. She turned on her heel and sprinted for home. When she arrived, she burst through the front door and took the stairs two at a time. She dashed into her room and dove under her bed, pulling out the dusty box and opening it, then carefully setting aside most of her treasured monster wrestling memorabilia.

Winnie found what she was looking for buried beneath old ticket stubs, souvenir programs, and photographs. She triumphantly removed her father's playbook—the real one—and clutched it to her chest, closing her eyes. The wisdom inside this book could make anyone a good coach. Add that to what Winnie already knew about monster wrestling, and she was sure to have a shot at bringing a monster to Stoker.

She tucked the book into her backpack and darted back down the stairs, running past her mother, who sat in her favorite chair working on a crossword puzzle.

"Bye, Mom!" Winnie shouted without slowing down. "I'm going to Pittsmore to find us a monster!"

"What!?" came her mom's voice just as Winnie made it out the front door.

Winnie didn't slow down until she reached the train station. She boarded a train and took a seat in a crowded car. As they pulled out of Stoker, she spotted workers removing the HOME OF TENTACULAR part of the WELCOME TO STOKER sign.

After a few hours and many stops, Winnie was the last passenger on the train. It was already dark when she stepped out at its final destination—Pittsmore. She stood on the run-down platform, under a flickering fluorescent light, as the train pulled away. When the tracks were clear, she spotted a huge factory nearby. The structure looked as if it had been abandoned years ago, yet bright lights flashed through its broken windows. The faint sound of a cheering crowd carried on the wind.

Winnie took in a deep breath before moving toward the abandoned factory turned underground fight club. The place looked terrifying, the complete opposite of the Jimbo Coyle Stadium back home. Every instinct told her to turn around, get back on the train, and go home. But Stoker was counting on her; she had to be brave.

She entered the building and moved through dark hallways, past piles of trash and graffiti-covered walls. The wrestling ruckus grew louder, so she knew she was heading in the right direction. Soon the ground vibrated beneath her feet, and thin trails of dust snaked down from the ceiling.

Winnie turned a corner and stepped into a cavernous main hall. Betting booths lined one side, while bars lined the other. In the center stood an enormous wrestling ring. Winnie could just make out movement in the ring, but the giant room was so crowded with spectators, she couldn't see who was fighting.

Winnie pushed her way through the crowd to get a better look. As she neared the ring, several audience members were shouting a monster's name.

"Axehammer! Axehammer!" they chanted.

When Winnie got to where she could see the match clearly, she saw what all the excitement was about. Axehammer was a vicious-looking monster with a mouth full of jagged teeth. She was covered in aquamarine scales and had a row of sharp orange spikes running down her spine. If that didn't make her scary enough, a long, sharp horn jutted from her snout and her whiplike tail ended in a fearsome spiked ball.

Axehammer was really giving it to her opponent, a four-eyed, gangly monster with striped fur and a long tail—not a spike or a horn on his entire body. The best thing about the monster was his long arms; they were the length of his entire body. He definitely had reach over Axehammer, but she never gave him a chance to use it. She wrapped her beefy arms around the thin monster and body-slammed him into the mat.

"Aw, come on, Nerdle," shouted a disappointed fan.

Axehammer placed a foot on Nerdle's back. "Come on!" she shouted. "Give me a challenge! Axehammer wants a challenge!"

"Ow!" Nerdle shouted.

Winnie dug out her father's playbook and began taking notes. This monster was fantastic!

"You want some more of that?" Axehammer asked. "You want some more of the Axehammer?"

The crowd cheered, but Nerdle shook his head. "No, no!"

Axehammer raised her arms, urging the audience to cheer louder. Then she leaped into the air and brought both feet down onto Nerdle's back.

Winnie cringed. "Ooooh!"

The audience roared, but Axehammer ramped them up even more. "Are you not entertained?" she asked with a hearty laugh.

"De-fen-e-strate! De-fen-e-strate!" the audience chanted back at her.

Axehammer grinned and picked up an anxious Nerdle. She whirled him around and around and around, until they were nothing more than a blur. Finally coming to a stop, she flung Nerdle out of the ring and above the crowd. The gangly monster kept going, crashing through a large window on the other side of the cavernous hall. The audience erupted in cheers as Axehammer flexed her muscles.

Winnie was thrilled with the horned monster. She was scary-looking, knew all the classic moves, was a great entertainer, and even had her own signature move. Winnie closed her father's playbook and smiled. She had found her monster.

Winnie pushed through the crowd, making her way to the monsters' large dressing room on the other side of the warehouse. Once inside, she climbed up the wobbly remains of an old scaffolding to be eye level with Axehammer herself. As the monster toweled off, Winnie explained every-thing that had happened in Stoker. She finished her long story by offering Axehammer a chance to be Stoker's official monster wrestler!

"It's an offer you can't refuse," Winnie said confi-dently. "That's right, you, Stoker, and me as your coach! It's a win-win-Winnie!" She was proud of that last line. There was no way Axehammer could turn down a pitch like that.

The spiked monster sipped from a giant sports bottle, eyeing Winnie carefully. She placed the bottle into her huge locker and slammed the door shut. Then she leaned close to Winnie, squinted her eyes, and burst into laughter.

Winnie's shoulders fell as the monster laughed and laughed and then laughed some more. Tears streamed down the monster's face as she literally roared with laughter. After what seemed like min-utes, Axehammer finally settled down, taking a deep breath and wiping her eyes.

"Oh, you are too much, sweetie," Axehammer said. "Does your mom even know you're here?"

Winnie sighed. So much for her perfect plan!

4
THE NOT-SO-PERFECT MONSTER

Winnie made the same exact pitch to several other monsters in the club. She tried to keep the same enthusiasm, but it was difficult when every monster laughed in her face. She even approached the smallest monster there—a furry, round ball with legs—named Denise. Even the fur ball, half the size of Axehammer, laughed at the offer.

Winnie finally gave up and sat at the bar. She drowned her sorrows in kombucha tea as the wrestling matches became more pitiful and the club slowly emptied for the night.

"So stupid," Winnie said as she struck her forehead with the heel of one palm. "What was I thinking? Like a monster was going to come back to Stoker with me." She shook her head in disgust. "Ugh!"

"Tough night, huh?" asked the man sitting beside her. The thin older man gave her a dismissive wave. "Don't worry. Your luck has to change, right?" He leaned back on his stool. "I mean, look at me. I just put every last cent I have on that guy!" He pointed to the ring.

Two monsters wrestled in the main ring. Well, two monsters were there, but only one looked as if he was actually wrestling. A blue warthog monster with a purple mohawk was beating the stuffing out of another monster.

"The guy with the tusks?" Winnie asked, pointing at the warthog. "He looks like a sure thing."

"Who, Klonk?" asked the man. He shook his head and pointed at the other wrestler. "No! The schlubby-looking guy with the horns."

"Ohhh," said Winnie. She turned her attention to the other monster. He was orange with yellow stripes, had two short horns on his head and stubby spikes running down his back, all the way to the tip of his long tail. He also had a large belly that jiggled with every move. He walked sluggishly and seemed out of breath after the simplest of motions.

"That there is Steve the Stupendous," the man explained.

Winnie couldn't think of anything nice to say about the unskilled wrestler. "Wow . . . he's . . ."

"Never won a single match!" the man finished. "He has a thousand-to-one odds. If he wins, I get a hundred grand!"

Winnie couldn't believe the man had bet everything he owned on such an obvious loser. Yet there was something oddly familiar about the monster. She couldn't be sure, but Winnie thought she had seen this monster before. She hopped off her stool and moved toward the ring.

As she closed in, Steve the Stupendous broke free from one of Klonk's holds. The orange monster then heaved himself up the ropes and stood on the turnbuckle, his back facing the ring. "Okay, you asked for it," Steve said over his shoulder as he swung his long tail back and forth. "Get ready for the Moon Boom!"

Winnie's mind was thrown back in time to when her father and Rayburn were still alive. Back then, she used to play with Rayburn's son, Rayburn Junior. The much younger and smaller monster had climbed the ropes and said that exact same thing. She pictured the shorter orange monster with yellow stripes standing on the turnbuckle in Stoker's training gym. He had swung his stubby tail out over the mat the same way.

"Get ready for the Moon Boom," Rayburn's son had said, before flinging himself, bottom-first, into the ring.

Back at the underground fight club, Winnie's eyes widened. "Rayburn Junior?" she muttered.

Steve the Stupendous pointed back at Klonk. "You're done for!"

Klonk snarled up at Steve. "Bring it on, you sack of warm puke."

Steve nodded. "Oh, I'm bringing the warm puke," he said with a laugh. He looked down at the mat and then back up at Klonk. "But I can't jump that far," he whispered.

"Boo!" shouted one of the few fans left in the place. "This stinks!"

"You stink!" Steve shouted back to the heckler. Then he motioned to Klonk. "Come closer."

"Rayburn Junior!" Winnie called up to him. "Is that you?"

"What?" the monster asked with wide eyes. He turned to see who had spoken to him. Unfortunately, he lost his balance and fell off the turnbuckle. "Dang it," Steve said as he hit the mat.

Klonk walked up to him and snorted in disgust. "Steve, come on man. What are you doing?" He leaned over the downed monster. "You're supposed to land on me," he whispered. "Then I reverse you back into the chicken-wing and then . . ."

Winnie was sure he was Rayburn Junior. "Hey, Ray-Ray!" she shouted, moving even closer. "Remember me?"

"Who is Ray?" asked Klonk.

"Uh, no one!" Steve said nervously. He sprang to his feet and grabbed Klonk around the waist. He dropped his legs and pushed the warthog down to the mat.

Winnie's eyes widened. "Whoa!"

"Did you see that!?" shouted the guy at the bar. "Yay, Steve!"

"What's going on, Steve?" Klonk asked, still pinned under him.

Steve chuckled. "Nothing. Just trying to mix it up a little bit."

The referee flew his hoverbike close to the wrestler's faces. "Stick to the script, fellas," he said. "We don't want to get the boss upset, do we?"

Both the monsters and the referee turned in unison. Winnie followed their gaze to a large door at the other side of the warehouse. A slit in the door opened, revealing a giant eye peering through. The eye blinked twice before the slit slid shut.

"No, we do not!" Steve said as he climbed off the warthog. "Okay, Klonk. Let's end this with a bang." He leaned forward and cupped a hand next to his mouth. "I'm going to go for the Kesagiri chop," he whispered. "But you catch it and then finish me off with a reverse clothesline," said Rayburn.

Klonk nodded and laughed. "Classic."

Winnie made it to the ring and climbed up the tall turnbuckle. She reached the top as the two monsters squared off.

"Rayburn!" Winnie shouted. She jumped up and down, waving her arms over her head. "Over here! It's me! Winnie Coyle. I know you see me."

Distracted, Steve/Rayburn turned toward Winnie just as Klonk was about to strike. The blue warthog missed Rayburn and slammed into the other turn-buckle. Stunned, he fell back onto the mat.

The referee hovered over to Winnie. "Hey, get off the ropes, kid!" he said. Then he turned to Rayburn. "Go down already."

"Got it!" Rayburn said.

Winnie couldn't believe Rayburn was ignoring her. She'd seen the way he glanced at her after she called his name. She knew she had the right monster. She scrambled off the turnbuckle and looked for a better way to get his attention.

Klonk slowly got to his feet, rubbing the back of his head. "What are you doing, Steve?"

"Sorry, buddy," Rayburn replied. "Just clothes-line me."

After the two monsters faced off, Rayburn threw Klonk into the ropes. The warthog sprang off them and ran back toward Rayburn.

That's when Winnie swung into the ring, dangling at the end of a long crane. "My dad coached your dad to eight straight championships!"

Rayburn turned and pushed the crane out of the way. "Would you get out of here?"

When he turned, Klonk missed him completely.

He ran by and bounced off the ropes on the other side of the ring.

Winnie swung back around. "You're Rayburn Junior! I know it!"

"I said get out of here!" Rayburn shouted, pushing the crane harder.

Unfortunately, Rayburn's arm was still out when Klonk came back around. The warthog slammed into Rayburn's stiff arm and flipped high into the air. He spun around once more before slamming to the mat.

BAM!

"Ah . . . ," Rayburn said, leaning over him. Klonk wasn't moving. The warthog was out cold.

"Oh no," said the referee as he flew down to Klonk's face. He lifted an eyelid to see a giant eye rolled back. The eyelid snapped closed when he let go. Not a good sign.

The referee swallowed hard and glanced nervously at the boss's door. "Uh . . . one . . . two . . ."

Rayburn frantically tried to prop up the unconscious monster. "Come on, Klonk," he said. "Get up, get up, get up!"

"Four . . . five . . . six . . ." The referee continued.

Rayburn even moved Klonk's arm to make it look as if he were punching him. "He's up. He's up."

"Seven . . . eight . . . nine . . ."

"Come on, Klonk," Rayburn said as he lay down on the mat next to Klonk. He tried to roll the other monster onto him.

"Nine and a half," stalled the referee. "Nine and three-quarters . . ."

Rayburn nervously glanced at the eye glaring through the slit in the boss's door before trying to lift the knocked-out Klonk.

"Nine and nine-tenths . . ." The referee shook his head. "Ten! Takedown! Fight's over!" He flew over to Rayburn and raised the monster's hand.

Rayburn jerked his hand away in terror.

Meanwhile, wild laughter erupted from the man at the bar. "I won! I won, I won!"

Winnie watched from the dangling crane as the boss's giant door creaked open. The few remaining spectators scattered as an enormous shadow filled the doorway.

"It was nice working with you, Steve," the referee said before he zoomed away on his hover-bike.

Klonk finally woke up and crawled out of the ring. "I'm out of here."

Rayburn backed away but tripped on the purple and white furry monster Winnie had spoken to earlier. Denise hopped up onto Rayburn's stomach and glared at him.

"Oh, hey, Denise," said Rayburn.

"Where do you think you're going, Steve?" Denise asked.

Rayburn shrugged. "Uh, nowhere?"

Everything in the warehouse shook as the biggest, scariest monster Winnie had ever seen stepped out of the shadows. The monster towered over everyone in the club, her blue feathers ruffling as she stomped forward. A sneer formed under her large, crooked beak, and her black eyes focused on Rayburn.

"Steve, Steve, Steve, Steve," she said in a sickly sweet voice. "Stevey-Stevey-Steve."

When she neared the ring, tiny leathery wings unfurled from her hunched back and beat wildly. They lifted her off the ground and set her gently onto the mat. She loomed over Rayburn.

"Looks like we have a little bit of a problem,

Stevey," she continued. "We have a little issue."

Rayburn wrung his hands. "It was an accident! I swear," he said. "You know me. I love to lose." He laughed nervously. "I'm the best loser in the biz! I'm the guy who loses!"

"Yes, you *were*," said the towering monster, before glancing toward the bar.

The man from earlier was laughing hysterically. "I won! I won a hundred grand! I can go to college now!"

The monster glared back at Rayburn. "Do you know what happens to those who betray Lady Mayhen?" She extended one of her bloodred talons and jabbed it under Rayburn's chin. "Very. Bad. Painful. Things." She pushed him back toward the ropes.

Denise bounced up from beside him. "Lady Mayhen wants her money."

"Listen, I'll make it up to you," Rayburn pleaded. "I'll wrestle for free! I'll clean the toilets! Even the monster toilets!"

Lady Mayhen shook her head. "You're embarrassing yourself, Steve."

Rayburn nodded as best he could with a sharp

talon under his chin. "Yes! I'll embarrass myself! Whatever you want!"

Lady Mayhen withdrew the talon and gave half a smile. "You know what I really want?" she asked, aiming the sharp claw at his forehead. "The money, honey. All of it. Times ten."

Rayburn scratched his head. "Honestly, I'm not great with math, but that sounds like a lot of money! I just don't know how I am ever going to pay you."

Winnie saw her moment. "I think I can help!" She leaped from the crane and landed atop Lady Mayhen's outstretched talon.

"I don't know you," Rayburn said, shaking his head at Winnie. Then he shook his head at Lady Mayhen. "I don't know her!"

"Sure you do!" said Winnie. "It's me. Winnie Coyle. Come on, you remember me, Raybur—"

"My name is Steve!" Rayburn interrupted.

"Hello?" Lady Mayhen asked. "I hate to interrupt this charming little reunion you're having, but there's still the matter of my money." She waved her hand about as she spoke. Winnie had to hold on for dear life to keep from being flung across the ring.

"I don't want to see you again until you have all of it. Every last dollar bill."

She flung Winnie onto Rayburn's head before flying away.

"Clock is ticking," Denise taunted before hopping after Lady Mayhen. "Ticktock, Steve. Ticktock."

Rayburn slumped as he watched them leave. Then he plucked Winnie from his head and placed her onto the mat before climbing out of the ring.

"Whoa!" Winnie shouted as she ran after him. "Hey! You up there! If you come with me to Stoker, I'll get you your money. All of it!"

Rayburn froze without looking back. "Stoker!?" He shook his head and kept walking.

Winnie chased after him as he marched toward the monster locker room. "No, no, no. Okay, so Tentacular turned heel and bailed," she said, giving the short version of her pitch. "You probably saw that along with everyone else in the world." Once in the locker room, Winnie climbed up a nearby scaffolding to get eye level with Rayburn. "So, the position of Stoker's official monster is wide open . . . fortunately for you!"

"Yeah. No!" Rayburn said. He swung open the locker door, blocking her from view.

"I'm not going back to"—he glanced around nervously—"to that place . . . where I've never been."

"Why are you doing this?" Winnie asked as she climbed through one of the vents of the locker door. "You have the DNA of a champion."

"Hey, kid," he said. "You have the wrong monster!"

Winnie laughed. "I don't think so, Rayburn."

Rayburn stiffened at the sound of his name. He glanced around again. "Will you knock that off?" he whispered.

Winnie cupped her hands around her mouth. "Rayburn, Rayburn, Rayburn, Rayburn, RAYBURN!"

The monster cringed with every mention of the name. "Rayburn was my dad," he said. "And I'm not gonna cash in on his name, ever."

Winnie pointed at him. "I knew it! I knew it was you! I mean, it's been forever, and I was like yea small"—she held her hand down low—"and you were like yea tall. . . ." She raised her hand higher.

"And now you're like yea wide. . . ." She spread both hands wide apart.

"Hey," Rayburn said, glancing down at his stomach. "You think monster puberty is easy?"

"Sorry," Winnie said. "But this is a real thing I'm offering you." She reached into her backpack and pulled out the playbook. "Look, I have my dad's playbook. I could coach you, get you a big match in Stoker and *boom*! Both our problems are solved!"

Rayburn's eyes widened. "You think you're going to coach me?" he asked before bursting into laughter. And much like with Axehammer, his laughs went on way too long.

Winnie's lips tightened, and she crossed her arms. His obviously fake laugh was very irritating.

"Oh, Stevey . . . ," came Lady Mayhen's voice.

That shut him up. He and Winnie glanced over to see the giant monster holding a squirming Klonk over her shoulder. "What are you still doing here?" she asked. "Go get me my money, man!"

"Help me," Klonk said before they disappeared into her office.

Rayburn turned back to Winnie and gave a nervous chuckle. "So, Coach . . . Stoker?"

5
GOING HOME

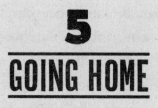

Rayburn stomped out of the club and into the night. He couldn't believe he was going along with this. Years ago, it took all his courage to run away from Stoker and leave his past behind. And now his past had just strolled into his club like it was no big deal and talked him into going back home. Rayburn shook his head in disgust. If he weren't so terrified of Lady Mayhen, he would tell Winnie to forget it and to forget him while she was at it.

Winnie huffed as she ran along beside him. "Isn't this great?" she asked. "It'll be just like old times again, you know!"

Rayburn rolled his eyes. "Pretty sure that doesn't mean the same thing to me as it does to you."

Winnie pulled ahead and climbed up an old, twisted crane. "Well, maybe you're not looking at it in the right way," she said when she was at eye level. "Maybe this is the change you need. An exciting new challenge! And the town is going to love—"

Rayburn held up a hand. " Stop talking."

He tromped away while she slid down a long cable to the ground. Rayburn heard her struggling to keep up as he marched across the countryside. *Good*, he thought. It served her right for dragging him all the way back to Stoker.

Rayburn didn't know why Winnie wanted to live in her father's shadow anyway. She was young and could do whatever she wanted with her life. She even had her own identity. Her name wasn't Jimbo Coyle Junior, after all. Rayburn didn't even have that going for him. He was Rayburn Junior, the son of Rayburn, the eight-time WMW Champion. Of course he had to change his name. That was the first thing he did after he ran away.

He stopped walking to let Winnie catch up to him. Without a word, he knelt and lowered a hand to the ground so she could step onto his palm. He didn't know if it was because she was out of breath, but thankfully, Winnie didn't start talking again when he placed her onto his head. He stood and continued his trek toward Stoker.

"Comfy up there?" he asked. "You must be exhausted from ruining my life. Need a pillow? Sorry, we don't provide turndown service."

Winnie didn't reply. She was already snoring.

Rayburn sighed and trudged on. He walked through the night and made it to Stoker just after dawn. Luckily, there weren't many people out as they moved through town. The town hadn't changed much, and even though he knew the way, Winnie directed him to the stadium. Seeing the looming structure after so many years gave him mixed feelings of excitement and dread. His stomach fluttered nervously as they made their way to the monster entrance in the back.

Rayburn pushed open the giant door to his father's old training gym. The room was cavernous, with monster-size punching bags, free weights, and jump ropes surrounding a huge sparring ring.

Winnie climbed down his body and hopped to the ground. She confidently strolled inside.

Rayburn put a foot forward to follow but froze.

"Here? Can't you find me an old mineshaft or abandoned nuclear power plant I can stay in?"

"Will you stop complaining?" Winnie asked. "This is perfect."

Rayburn sighed and stepped inside. Once his eyes adjusted, he couldn't help but look around. He gazed at the old wrestling posters plastered across one wall, along with trophies and photos from his father's glory days.

"Wow," he said, running a hand over a familiar repair in an old punching bag. "This place hasn't changed a bit."

Rayburn spotted his old weight set. He picked up a dumbbell, which was now tiny in his hand. He turned it over to see a sticker that read RAY JR. CHAMP.

"It's magical, isn't it?" Winnie asked. She spun around and took in a deep breath. "It's still got that smell of sweat . . . and feet. Really big feet."

"You're a weird kid," he said with a chuckle. "Real weird."

"Come on," Winnie said. "Don't you feel like you're finally home?"

Rayburn didn't answer. Instead, he stared at the

giant mural of his father on the back wall behind the ring. Muscles rippling, his long horns sharpened, his father seemed to stare back at him with a confident grin.

A ten-year-old memory flooded into his mind. Rayburn remembered being in that very ring, dancing in front of his father, Coach Jimbo, Siggy, and even a six-year-old Winnie. Rayburn remembered having the time of his life, trying out dance moves he had picked up from all over the world.

Jimbo had laughed and nudged Rayburn Senior. "Your boy's got some moves, Ray."

"That doesn't look like wrestling," young Winnie had added with a frown.

"See? Even the girl knows," said Siggy. "You have to set your kid straight, Ray. Monsters wrestle; they don't dance."

"Okay, okay," his dad had said. "Enough messing around, kiddo. Siggy's right." He ushered Rayburn Junior out of the ring. "If you want to be a champ like me, you gotta get serious!"

The memory faded, and Rayburn glanced around the gym nervously. "This was a mistake. I gotta get out of here."

"Wait, what?" Winnie asked with wide eyes.

Rayburn was about to go for the door when he heard the voices of people approaching.

"No, I'm telling you," a woman said. "Winnie had a monster! She did it!"

"Was it big?" asked a man.

"Something scary, I hope," said another woman.

"Did it have a spiky tail? Or wings?" asked another man. "I love those."

The voices grew louder as twenty people filed into the gym. Rayburn fidgeted, backing toward the ring.

"Maybe I won't have to sell my hair salon!" said a woman.

"Maybe I'll get reelected!" said a man in a sports coat.

"Maybe I'll—oh!" said a man. Everyone froze when they saw Rayburn by the ring.

"Well," said a woman. "Technically it's a monster."

The crowd moved closer, looking Rayburn up and down. He shifted uncomfortably under their probing gaze.

"Maybe he has electro breath, like Sparkaiju," added a man. "Or he can grow armor plates, or . . .

57

shoot eye beams or something. Hopefully."

The man in the sports coat turned to the others. "Maybe he has a great coach!"

Winnie stepped between Rayburn and the people. She proudly placed her hands on her hips. "You're looking at her!"

"Winnie?" asked the sports coat guy. "You're coaching . . . that?"

A woman threw up her hands in disgust. "Guess I'm selling the hair salon."

"Guys! This is the solution to all our problems." Winnie pointed back at Rayburn. "Right here!"

Rayburn smiled and sat on the edge of the ring, leaning back on the lowest rope.

"Who needs Tentacular," Winnie continued. "When we have . . . Steve! The! Stupendous!"

Rayburn gave a small wave. The people simply gawked back at him, confused.

A thin woman scratched her head. "Stupendous at what, exactly?"

"Okay, everybody," Winnie said. "I know he might not look like much."

"He looks kind of squidgy," said a woman.

Rayburn frowned. "Hey!"

"That's not what I meant," Winnie explained. "Look . . ." She pointed back at Rayburn. "Steve has a champion monster inside him!"

"Did he . . . eat one?" asked a young boy.

Everyone burst into laughter.

Rayburn shook his head and got to his feet. "Hey, you know what? You guys are rude. I'm outta here."

Winnie ran up to him. "No, no, no, wait!" She slipped off her backpack and reached inside. She pulled out an old book and held it above her head. "This is Coach Jimbo's playbook. It has every trick, every move—everything my dad knew is in here. I can use it to train Steve."

"That's great, sweetheart," said a woman in overalls. "But you're not your dad."

Winnie's lips tightened as the people turned to leave. Then she opened the book and flipped through some pages. "Just wait. It's all right here."

Rayburn glanced down to see that she stopped on a page titled THE SPEECH—A COACH'S SECRET WEAPON.

Winnie cleared her throat and lowered the book. "Okay, look. This is about right here, right now. Because . . ." Beads of sweat formed on her forehead. "People, this . . . this is that moment we'll look back on . . . on . . ." Winnie shook her head. "Oh, nuts . . ." Her eyes widened, and she shook her head. "Not nuts. The moment. We'll look back on this moment, you know, in the future, at some point, and we're going to say that moment in the past, where we did the thing . . . that is now. That in the future, so . . . cool!"

The townspeople stared back at her with confused expressions. Then they turned to leave, grumbling as they went.

"Come on, don't go!" Winnie pleaded. "I can do this!"

"That was your inspirational coach speech?" Rayburn asked. "I wasn't humiliated enough already?"

Winnie gazed up at him. "Steve . . ."

Rayburn grabbed both sides of his head and clenched his eyes shut. "I'm so dead. Mayhen is gonna find me. Then she's gonna, I don't know, eat me or something."

Rayburn opened his eyes to see that one of the townspeople had stayed behind. He recognized the woman right away.

"Hi, Mom," Winnie said.

Her mother gestured up at Rayburn. "Steve the Stupendous?"

"Don't you recognize him?" Winnie asked excitedly. "That's Rayburn Junior."

Rayburn gave her a nervous wave. "Hey, Mrs. C."

Winnie's mother squinted up at Rayburn for a couple of seconds before her eyes widened with recognition. "Wow," she said. "Monster puberty was rough."

"Okay!" barked Rayburn as he threw up his hands. "Thanks for the stroll down memory lane."

Rayburn marched to the back of the gym. He thought about starting back for Pittsmore right away. After all, he didn't have to sit there and be insulted. He could be insulted just fine back at the underground fight club like he always was. At least there he wouldn't have photos and murals of his father staring down at him while it happened.

The trouble was, he couldn't really go back to Pittsmore, could he? He couldn't even show his face there without Lady Mayhen's money. He racked his brain trying to think of ways to pay back Mayhen. Except there weren't many jobs out there for monster wrestlers who specialized in losing. And even if he found another underground fight club, and if they paid him *close* to what Mayhen had paid him, it would take the rest of his life to pay off his debt.

Winnie found him in the back of the gym. "Hey, when life knocks you down, you get right back up."

Rayburn's shoulders slumped. "Maybe you ought to try staying down." He gave half a smile. "It's a lot easier."

"Yeah, well," Winnie said, squinting up at him, "that's not going to get you the money you need, is it?"

Rayburn raised an eyebrow. "You really think you can get me a paid match?"

Winnie nodded confidently. "I know I can!"

Rayburn leaned forward. He almost went for it before coming to his senses. He shook his head. "No, I'm not . . ." He pointed at her. "This isn't . . . It's never going to work."

But how else was he going to get the money?

After a few more seconds of internal struggle, Rayburn roared with frustration. "Fine!" He bent down and pointed at Winnie. "But I'm doing it for the money! Not for some stadium or unresolved feelings about my father or because I feel bad for you. You got me?"

"Yep." Winnie nodded. "Got it. Money all the way. Deal?"

Rayburn sighed. "Fine. Deal."

"Okay. Get some beauty sleep," Winnie ordered.

Rayburn howled with laughter. He held his bouncing belly, chortling at the funniest thing he had ever heard. His guffaws quickly faded, however, when he caught the determined look in Winnie's eyes.

Oh, wait, he thought. *She's serious!*

6
RUDE AWAKENING

The next morning, Winnie's hand was lightning fast as she switched off her roaring monster alarm clock. She was wide-awake as she leaped out of bed and threw on her clothes. She brushed her teeth with one hand while gathering her coaching materials with the other. She shoved the playbook and other plans into her backpack and threw on her dad's old coaching cap. Unfortunately, it fell over her eyes, too big. Winnie adjusted the cap and happily put it on again. This was going to be a great day!

As she headed toward the door, she stopped and stared at a framed magazine cover. It showed her father, wearing the same cap, confidently smiling at the camera. Winnie's eyes shifted from the magazine cover to the nearby mirror. She didn't see a world-famous monster wrestling coach. She saw a little girl in an oversize hat *pretending* to be a coach.

Winnie threw down the pack. "I can't do this," she said, shaking both hands nervously. "What am I doing? Look at me!" She cringed when she glanced at the mirror again.

She began to hyperventilate as she fluttered around the room in full-blown panic mode. "This is insane! I don't look like a coach! I've never coached anything!" She wrung her hands together. "What am I doing?"

There was a knock at her bedroom door.

"Good morning," her mother said as she opened the door. "How're you feeling? You ready?"

Winnie plopped down on the bed. "Do you think I can do this?"

Her mom sat and put an arm around her. "I think you won't know until you try."

Winnie leaned against her mother and sighed.

Her mother gave her shoulder a squeeze. "You don't train the monster you wish you had. You train the one you've got."

Winnie perked up. "Did Dad say that?"

Her mother chuckled. "No. Mom did. When your father complained about working with some nobody wrestler named Rayburn Senior."

Winnie felt a spark of hope ignite inside her. Did her father really have self-doubt too? And he turned out to be the greatest monster wrestling coach of all time! Winnie swelled with pride and renewed confidence as she got to her feet.

"You forgetting something?" her mother asked. She stood and reached into her pocket, pulling out something jingly and tossing it to Winnie.

Winnie opened her hand to see the keys to her father's hoverbike. "Dad's keys," she said with amazement.

Her mother nodded. "You tell Rayburn . . . I mean Steve . . . that his Aunt Maggie says *hi*. Now go coach him." She raised an eyebrow. "He looks like he needs it."

Winnie dashed over and kissed her mother on the cheek. "Thanks, Mom!" Then she squealed in delight as she snatched up her backpack and zipped out the door.

Winnie ran to the stadium's museum alcove and started up the gleaming hoverbike. It roared to life as if it had been running only yesterday. Although the gym was below the stadium, Winnie couldn't help but take the bike on a quick victory lap around the town.

Once she got that out of her system, she parked the bike inside the gym and hopped off. Rayburn snored loudly as he slept under his father's mural.

"Steve, you ready?" she asked as she marched across the gym. The monster continued to snore.

Winnie gently pushed on his giant shoulder. "Hey . . . rise and shine." She peeked around his horn, but his eyes were still shut tight.

Winnie finally cupped her hands around her mouth and took in a deep breath. "Rayburn, wake up!" she shouted into his ear.

"What!?" Rayburn said as he shot up. He shook his head. "I had this terrible dream that I promised I would get up and train." He glanced down at Winnie. "Oh, it's real."

"So, are you ready?" Winnie asked. She hopped up and down. "Let's do this!"

"You go ahead," Rayburn replied as he lay back down. "You start. Set up the cones or whatever."

"Oh, no you don't!" Winnie tried to grab

Rayburn's arm. "Up and at 'em, sunshine. It is go time! Game day! No time like the present." She finally let go. She couldn't keep him vertical and she couldn't think of more sports clichés.

Rayburn cracked one eye. "You are a rude little girl."

"Scooch your booty!" Winnie shouted. She ran behind him and pushed on his back. It felt like pushing against a brick wall, but she kept at it. "This is Important with a capital *I*!"

"Yeah, well, I never thought training was all that important," Rayburn mumbled.

Winnie paused to catch her breath. "I can tell." She gave one last shove. "No one thinks we can do this, but we're going to show them!"

Rayburn rolled over to face her. As he grinned, she thought she was finally getting through to him. "I'm going back to sleep now," he said, shutting his eyes.

"You just get me that match," he said without opening his eyes. "I'll take care of the rest."

Winnie stepped back and blew a stray strand of hair from her face. She remembered Rayburn Junior being so happy and full of energy. But he grew up to be the slowest, laziest, most out-of-shape monster she had ever seen. She thought she could train him to be great, but how could she stand a chance if he wouldn't even try? There had to be some way to motivate the sluggish monster.

"Okay," Winnie said with a wide grin. "I'll get you a match."

7

THIS IS WINNING?

Rayburn let out a big toothy yawn. He and Winnie had spent most of the day traveling a couple of towns over. He could probably take a nap right then if he wanted to. What stopped him was the fact that he was in the middle of a wrestling ring about to start a match. Plus, all the screaming monster wrestling fans would probably keep him up. Of course, they weren't cheering for him.

True to her word, Winnie had gotten him a lower-league match down by the docks. Rayburn sat in his corner of the ring and glanced around the arena for his opponent. The giant wrestling stadium was made out of shipping containers surrounded by tanker trucks on one side and cargo ships on the other. The venue wasn't quite as seedy as the factory in Pittsmore, but it was close. However, Winnie had assured him that this was an official circuit match. She stood atop his turnbuckle, her hoverbike floating nearby.

"Welcome, everyone, to an evening of monster wrestling," boomed the announcer's voice. "Weighing in at eighteen tons! You know him. You love him. You're scared of him. Wham-Bam, Ramarilla Jackson!"

A silhouetted figure leaped across several cargo ships and shipping containers. After one final jump, he somersaulted in midair before slamming into the ring. The monster was a ferocious gorilla with giant ram's horns on his head.

"Here comes the rammer-hammer!" Ramarilla shouted. He raised both arms and addressed the crowd. "Ramma-Ramma-Ramma!"

"Rilla, rilla, rilla!" answered the crowd.

"Boom! Boom!" Ramarilla beat his chest and leaped out of the ring. "It's Ramarilla time!" He grabbed two oil tankers and smashed himself over the head with them.

"Oof!" Rayburn cringed. "Talk about anger issues."

Winnie took a deep breath and began pacing back and forth. "Okay. *Webster's Dictionary* defines 'tenacity' as—"

Rayburn waved his hands. "Whoa, whoa, whoa. Time out! What are you doing?"

"I'm doing my coach speech," Winnie replied.

"You think that's a good idea?" Rayburn asked. "Given your track record?"

Winnie sighed. "Fine. Then let's talk strategy." She held up the playbook and pointed to a page covered in diagrams. "You want to fake a Reverse Saito, and then when we get him behind you . . ."

"Uh-huh . . . ," Rayburn replied, not really listening. After a few more seconds, he finally cut her off. "You know what? I think I'm going to go with what I know."

"Uh, no." Winnie shook her head. "I'm your coach, and we need a strategy."

Rayburn waved her away. "Trust me. I got this."

Ramarilla slammed back into the ring and joined the referee in the center. "Watch and learn," Rayburn told her as he stepped out to join them.

"You know the rules," said the referee as he floated on his hoverbike. "I want a good, clean wrestling match. So if you're going to do something illegal, don't let me see it. Go to your corners and come out wrestling."

"But not *too* hard, right?" Rayburn told Ramarilla with a nervous chuckle. "Sorry, I love to laugh. That's me."

"Oh, I ain't laughing," Ramarilla said, leaning closer. "But I will be when I pin your face in the dirt and break your tail with my horns."

Rayburn smiled nervously as he returned to his corner. "Can't wait."

The bell rang, and the wrestlers stepped toward each other. Rayburn did his best to put on a scary monster face.

"And here come the wrestlers, circling each other," said the announcer's voice.

Ramarilla charged, swinging a long arm toward Rayburn. A giant, meaty gorilla fist just missed Rayburn's face.

"Gosh, you really got me on that," Rayburn said, pretending to be hit by the blow. He stumbled back. "I think I'm knocked out." He swooned. "I'm going down. . . ." Rayburn stiffened and fell straight back. "Timmmberrrrr . . ." He slammed onto the mat.

The referee flew down beside Rayburn's head. "One . . . two . . . three . . ."

"What are you doing?" Winnie asked.

Rayburn didn't move. He lay flat on his back, making his best knocked-out face—mouth open, eyelids half-open with his eyes rolled back. He even stuck his tongue out a bit as an added touch.

Ramarilla stomped over to him. "Get up, drama queen!"

Rayburn remained perfectly still as the referee kept counting. If there was one thing he learned from his vast career of losing, it was to hold perfectly still for the count of ten.

"I know you can hear me, you big faker!" Ramarilla yelled. "Get up so I can knock you out!"

"Don't you think that's kind of a waste?" Rayburn murmured back to him, still trying to remain frozen. "I mean, I'm already down here and everything."

"Seven . . . ," continued the referee. "Eight . . . nine . . ."

Ramarilla leaned close to the referee and snarled. "Stop right there or you're next." The referee backed away.

Rayburn opened his eyes a bit as the gorilla jumped into the air. He flew higher and higher, until he was a tiny silhouette in front of the moon.

Rayburn whistled in amazement. "Wow. You're really up there, huh?"

Then he watched in horror as Ramarilla rocketed back down, one of his giant feet aimed at Rayburn's face.

"No, no, no, no, no!" Rayburn said as he rolled to the side in the nick of time. The huge gorilla slammed to the mat inches from his head.

Ramarilla roared with rage. He pounded his chest before charging forward.

This guy was serious. There was no way Rayburn could fake his way out of this one. He put his hands over his head and slammed his eyes shut.

Ding-ding!

"And that's round one," said the announcer.

Ramarilla snorted in disgust as he marched to his corner. Rayburn, shocked that he was still alive, slinked to his own corner.

Winnie stood on the turnbuckle, waiting for him. "What was that?" she asked. "This isn't the

Underground. You don't get to throw matches in the league."

Rayburn nodded. "Yeah, I get that now." He clapped his hands together and looked across at Ramarilla. "Okay, I just need to figure out how to not die and then *cha-ching*!" He smiled at Winnie. "That's the sound of me making money."

"Oh, uh . . . ," she said, fidgeting. "Thing is, there is no money."

"Wait, what?" Rayburn threw up his hands. "You said this was a paid match."

"It is," she replied. "Winner takes all. You didn't read the paperwork I had you sign?"

Rayburn shook his head. "Nobody reads the paperwork!"

"So, if you want that money, we're gonna have to try a radical new strategy here." Winnie leaned forward. "Ready for it? Try . . . to . . . win!"

Rayburn sighed. "Okay, big shot. How?"

Winnie squinted across the ring. "Okay, uh . . . so he's strong. . . ."

"Yeah," Rayburn replied. "Got that."

"He's freakishly strong," she added. "But you know what that means. . . . No stamina. So here's

what you're going to do." She leaned forward as if letting him in on a big secret. "Run away."

"Uh-huh," Rayburn said, raising an eyebrow.

"If he does catch you, let him hit you," Winnie added. "Then start running again!"

Rayburn crossed his arms. "That's your big plan?"

"Yup," Winnie replied. "And then, when he's all punched out, we make our move."

"So, run away, and then let him hit me, huh?" Rayburn asked, rubbing his chin. "Actually sounds like something I can do."

The bell rang for round two, and Ramarilla charged. Luckily, as planned, Rayburn was able to get out of the way at the last second. Furious, the gorilla skidded to a stop and spun around. He charged again.

"Oh no!" Rayburn shouted as he ran around the ring. The angry gorilla galloped after him.

"Okay, so now what?" Rayburn asked Winnie as he passed her turnbuckle "Just keep going in a circle and hope he runs out of steam?"

"Yes!" she replied. "That's it! Keep going! You're doing it!"

Rayburn led the gorilla on a chase around the ring, but Ramarilla showed no signs of slowing down. In fact, he seemed to get angrier with every turn.

"I thought you said he had no stamina!" Rayburn shouted. Meanwhile, Rayburn found it harder to breathe. He panted heavily, but Ramarilla seemed to be as fresh as he was when he had arrived.

Rayburn had to do something different. As he came back around, he spotted a crane's hook dangling over them. He jumped up and grabbed it, his momentum swinging him over the ropes and out of the ring.

"See you later, suckers!" Rayburn said with a laugh. He let go and smashed into a stack of large shipping containers. "Oh, that smarts," he said as giant metal boxes tumbled everywhere.

As Rayburn scrambled to his feet, Ramarilla leaped out of the ring and burst through the remaining containers.

Rayburn put one foot onto a flatbed train car and used it like a giant skateboard. He pushed off with the other foot, gaining some speed. He skated down the docks, weaving around tall stacks of shipping containers.

On her hoverbike, Winnie pulled up next to him. "Keep it up! He's slowing down!"

"Is he!?" Rayburn glanced back at the pursuing gorilla. Ramarilla's eyes were aflame with rage as he thundered after them. "Because it feels like he's speeding up!"

"Look out!" Winnie warned.

Rayburn looked ahead just as he ran into another dangling crane hook. It snagged one of his horns and the machine swung him out in a wide arc. He fell loose from the crane to land atop a tall stack of shipping containers. Breathing heavily, he crouched low, hiding from his pursuer.

Ramarilla turned a corner, his chest heaving as he glanced around. Then he looked up and spotted Rayburn. The gorilla lowered his head and charged forward.

BAM!

The containers shook beneath Rayburn's feet as Ramarilla rammed the one on the bottom, causing the stack to slowly fall over. Rayburn struggled to keep his balance. At the last second, he leaped onto another nearby tower of containers. But they were struck by the first one and began to fall over too.

Rayburn hopped across several stacks as they fell like dominos beneath his feet.

"No, no, no, no!" Rayburn shouted, running across the toppling containers. "Does he just not get hurt? Is that his deal?"

When Rayburn reached the final stack, he leaped off, into thin air. Arms and legs flailing, he snagged another crane hook at the last second.

"Ahhhhhh!" Rayburn yelled as he swung around in a wide arc. It brought him back to the ring and slammed him against a turnbuckle. He fell back into the center of the ring, dazed and seeing double.

Two Winnies flew up to him. "Get up!" they ordered. "He's coming!"

As Rayburn's vision began to clear, he spotted Ramarilla staggering toward the ring. Rayburn mustered all of his strength to crawl toward his opponent. Ramarilla dragged himself into the ring and wriggled closer. The two monsters met, lying next to each other. Exhausted, they gasped for air as they traded weak, feeble blows.

Ramarilla reared back for a final, massive blow. Instead, he kept falling backward until he landed on his back, completely spent.

"Now!" Winnie shouted. "Pin him!"

Rayburn slowly crawled atop the massive gorilla. "I . . . am less . . . exhausted . . . than you." He collapsed atop Ramarilla.

The referee flew down to Ramarilla's face. "He's out!" the ref shouted.

"And the winner is . . . Steve the Stupendous!" said the announcer. The referee raised Rayburn's hand.

"Yes!" Winnie shouted. "Way to go Ray . . . Steve!"

Wait . . . had he actually won?

Suddenly, Rayburn was wide-awake. "Oh yeah!" he shouted, springing to his feet. The mat thundered beneath him as he broke into a victory dance. He held a hand out to Winnie's hoverbike and she hopped on.

"You did it," she told him. "You won!"

Rayburn couldn't help but smile. "This is winning?"

"Yeah!" Winnie replied. "How does it feel?"

Rayburn widened his grin as he looked at the cheering crowd. Usually, he heard cheering while he lay in the ring, pretending to be knocked out. It was strange being vertical as the audience applauded . . . for him.

"It feels . . . not bad," Rayburn replied with a chuckle as he listened to the cheers. "Not bad at all!"

8
SECRET SALSA

The next day, Winnie rode on Rayburn's shoulder as he strolled through the streets of Stoker. She was thrilled about their win the night before, but she knew they had a lot of work ahead of them.

"So, let's break down what we learned," she said. "On the plus side, we won."

"Yay me," Rayburn said as he halfheartedly pumped a fist into the air.

"On the minus side," Winnie continued. "We are not very good."

"And for just the tiniest moment there I was feeling okay about myself," Rayburn said.

As they reached the stadium, Winnie caught herself gazing longingly at its grand entrance. She could almost hear the cheers as Rayburn strolled toward the ring. She pictured herself riding next to him on her hoverbike. Both of them moving beneath the Jimbo and Rayburn Senior banners, beneath the encouraging eyes of their fathers.

Winnie realized that Rayburn had stopped walking. He too stared silently at the marble monument of their past.

Winnie snapped out of her daydream. "We're nowhere near getting a match there. Let alone filling it up and stopping Jimothy," she said. "And you've barely put a dent in your debt. We need to get serious."

Rayburn nodded and marched around to the gym entrance. Once inside, he gently placed Winnie on the floor. She ran to her backpack and pulled out her father's playbook.

"It's time to do it by the book, my dad's playbook," she said, pointing to the worn volume. "This is the key that'll turn you from a zero into a hero."

"Oh, *zero*, is it?" Rayburn asked. He rolled his eyes. "That's motivating."

Winnie flipped through the pages. "Chapter one. Basic Fitness."

Rayburn glanced down at his large stomach. "Ugh, I'm tired already."

"Yeah!" Winnie shouted, trying to get some momentum going. "Let's do this!" She pulled out her phone and remotely switched on the gym's stereo. The small boom box thumped out a driving beat, perfect for exercising. Winnie was ready to train!

Unfortunately, Rayburn was not.

The out-of-shape monster couldn't do a single push-up. He couldn't lift a single free weight. And when she took him to a nearby bridge, Rayburn couldn't even do one simple pull-up.

After a few hours of her monster failing to train, Winnie switched off the stereo.

"I don't understand," she said, thumbing through the playbook. "We've got the right music playing and everything. You should be getting better."

Rayburn rubbed his belly. "Probably should have gone lighter on breakfast."

"Yes, you should have," Winnie agreed. "We're going to work on your diet later."

She had to find another approach. "Let's go to the tape," she said, pressing a button on her phone. The gym's large television screen snapped on, showing an old wrestling match where Rayburn Senior dominated his opponent.

Winnie had seen this match hundreds of times. She excitedly pointed at the screen. "Look, look, look!" she squealed. "Right there! The Reverse Saito! It can't be defended."

Rayburn sighed. "Are you really going to show me film of my dad?"

"Of course," she replied. "He's the greatest."

The monster shook his head in disbelief. "Yeah, that's the last thing I need. Have you never heard of daddy issues?"

Winnie winced. "Oh, right. Sorry." She switched off the screen.

Rayburn groaned. "This is why I left Stoker. I'm never going to be my dad, okay?" He plopped to the ground, slumped in defeat.

Winnie looked at Rayburn and then at all the memorabilia plastered around the gym. Rayburn Senior was everywhere. There were fight posters, photographs with celebrities, product endorsements. . . . No wonder Rayburn was so intimidated.

"Okay, maybe you're right," she said, slamming the book shut. "Maybe I'm going about this all wrong." She walked over and sat beside him. "What is it that *Steve* loves to do?"

Rayburn seemed to consider the question. "Uhhhh . . . nothing."

"Come on!" Winnie bumped his side. "There must be something."

"No, I'm sorry," Rayburn said. "I literally mean . . . I like to do nothing."

Winnie raised an eyebrow. "I'm going to need more than that."

"Oh . . ." Rayburn thought for a moment. "Uh, sleeping?"

"Really?" asked Winnie.

"Yeah!" Rayburn's face lit. "I'm really good at it." He snapped his fingers. "Or . . . sitting is another one. I like sitting!"

Winnie closed her eyes and slowly shook her head. "Not helping."

Rayburn rubbed his chin. "Did I mention sitting? I feel like I did." His eyes widened. "Oh! Eating!"

Winnie rolled her eyes. "Is there anything else?"

"Oh, there's also salsa," he said quietly. "But uh, yeah, that's it. That's probably it."

"Like, with chips?" asked Winnie. "Or like

salsa–salsa?" She stood and made a few dance steps.

Rayburn shook his head and laughed nervously. "What? No . . . I don't like . . . dancing."

Winnie pulled out her phone. "Is that so?" She scrolled through her selection of music before switching on the stereo. Suddenly, a brisk Latin beat flowed from the speakers.

Winnie crossed her arms and stared at Rayburn. For a moment the monster merely sat there. Then, slowly at first, his head began to bob back and forth. His shoulders rose and fell as his foot tapped along with the beat. Rayburn finally sprang to his feet and began dancing.

"Okay, yes!" he growled. He swayed his hips, keeping his knees together and holding a hand against his stomach. "There's nothing on this planet I love more than dancing!" He held out the other arm as if dancing with an invisible partner. "You know, this is merengue music, not salsa," he explained before going into a spin. "But I love all Latin dances."

Winnie backed away, giving the twenty-two-ton twirler some room. She had never seen a monster dance before and covered her eyes with embarrassment. But then, after peeking through her fingers, she noticed his nimble footwork, fluid motion, and precise movements.

"You're a surprisingly good dancer," said Winnie.

Rayburn arched his back and gave a high kick. "I ran with a pretty fast crowd in Cuba when my dad wrestled down there." His feet were a blur as he ran through the steps, double time.

Winnie's eyes widened. "Wrestling is eighty percent footwork," she whispered. She opened the playbook and riffled through the pages.

Rayburn didn't hear her; he was in the zone— the dance zone. "I learned the tango in Argentina, the flamenco in Spain. . . ." He threw his arms wide as he spun. "Anyway, that was a different life."

"Hold on," Winnie said, scanning the pages.

"How about this?" Rayburn asked, leaping high into the air. He landed gracefully in a split. "Not bad for twenty-two tons."

Winnie barely saw the big finish. Instead, her eyes focused on a footwork diagram in her father's playbook. A bunch of Xs and Os covered the page, telling the wrestler where to step. Winnie imagined those markings on the gym floor, showing Rayburn where to step . . . where to dance step!

9
ON THE DOWNBEAT

The audience cheered inside the dark Central American arena. For the final match of the evening, Rayburn stood in the ring across from the local favorite, Lucho Luchon. The masked monster was covered in blue and green scales, had four legs, two wiry arms, and a mane of feathers fanning out from behind his horns. The long lizard grinned a sharp, toothy grin at Rayburn from across the ring.

For the first time ever, Rayburn was nervous before a match. His bouts in Pittsmore had all been carefully choreographed, with him always losing the match in the end. He hadn't been anxious before his bout with Ramarilla because he had planned to lose that match too. Now, however, Rayburn was beginning a wrestling match with the goal of winning.

What was he thinking!?

"Lucho! Lucho! Lucho!" chanted the crowd.

Winnie stood behind him atop the turnbuckle. Rayburn sighed and looked down at her. "Are you sure this is going to work?"

Winnie shrugged and gave a half smile. "We won't know until we try."

For the past week, Winnie had helped Rayburn combine his smooth dance steps with classic wrestling moves. She had even made giant monster-size footprints and laid them out all over the gym floor. Rayburn had learned the new moves and drilled them over and over again. Now he hoped all of their practice would pay off.

The bell rang, and Rayburn danced to the center of the ring. Spicy salsa music played in his head as his feet moved rhythmically to the beat. Rayburn's chest swelled with pride. He could actually pull this off!

Lucho Luchon looked down at Rayburn's footwork and sneered. After that, all Rayburn saw was a teal blur. The lizard moved at lightning speed, seeming to attack from every direction at once. Rayburn bounced around the ring under all the blurry blows.

"Ahhh!" Rayburn shouted as he was slammed back into his turnbuckle.

"Oof!" Winnie winced before forcing a smile. "You're doing great!"

Rayburn stepped out and raised his hands, preparing another dance move. That was when, out of nowhere, Lucho delivered a flutter of kicks to his face. He was spun back into his turnbuckle.

Rayburn wobbled on his feet and raised his fists. "All right . . . where is he?"

Lucho snaked up the turnbuckle behind him and leaped off. He smashed into Rayburn, slamming him to the ground. Then he whirled him around the ring, bouncing him off the ropes before clotheslining him.

Rayburn stumbled to his feet. He felt beaten emotionally as well as physically. For once, he had dared to have hope. But against someone like Lucho, all of the training had been for nothing.

"I can't even see him," Rayburn told Winnie. "This guy is crazy fast!"

Lucho, who had been showing off for the cheering crowd, set his sights back on Rayburn. He hunched forward and moved in.

"You've got to slow him down," Winnie said. "Tango, tango, tango!"

A lone violin played in Rayburn's mind as he began to dance the tango. This time, when Lucho zipped in for another attack, Rayburn snagged one of his arms and pulled him in close. Lucho's eyes widened as Rayburn squeezed him tight and danced with him across the ring.

"That's it!" Winnie yelled. "You got it!"

Lucho struggled to break free, but Rayburn held tight. Then, on the downbeat, Rayburn twirled Lucho, spinning him faster and faster. When he finally released Lucho, the thin monster ricocheted around the ring like a pinball.

The dizzy lizard bounced off the ropes and back into Rayburn's arms. With an elegant flourish, Rayburn lowered Lucho into a deep dip. Then he dropped the lizard to the mat. He flung himself on top of Lucho, pinning him for the win!

Rayburn couldn't believe it. Their dancing wrestling moves actually worked!

10
DANCE DANCE EVOLUTION

Winnie was thrilled with their latest win. It was proof that Rayburn's wrestling style, although unconventional, was the real deal. She could tell that Rayburn was excited because he actually began to take training a little more seriously. Unfortunately, she still had a tough time waking him up in the morning.

One morning she'd climbed onto his chest and pushed his face around. "Hey!" she had shouted. "Rayburn, wake up! Come on!"

Another morning, she'd actually stood on his face and yelled at him through a megaphone. "Are you pretending to be asleep right now?" she had asked him. "Get up, Rayburn!"

What had finally worked was when she had blasted him with a fire hose—from a safe distance, of course. Rayburn's limbs flailed as he snorted and sputtered under the cold stream. "I'm awake. I'm awake!"

Winnie had Rayburn running on the gym's huge monster-size treadmill as well as through the town of Stoker itself. While he huffed and sweated through every step, Winnie followed behind him on her hoverbike. Like any good coach, she made sure to shout out encouraging words along the way. "Come on, push it!" she had shouted. "Pain is just weakness leaving the body!"

Rayburn was getting in better shape every day. It wasn't long before he could do more than one push-up and pull-up.

However, Rayburn's real improvement came through his dance moves. Together, Winnie and Rayburn adapted more wrestling moves into rumbling rumbas, hip-hop hits, and ballet beat-downs.

One of his new moves featured a one-two swing dance move where he hip-checked a punching bag on the downbeat before swiping another bag with his tail.

"Bravo!" Winnie yelled as she clapped.

Once they had perfected that move, they had used it in the bout against the ferocious wrestling twins. Even though the monsters were half Rayburn's size, the snarling little beasts were full of intensity and teeth.

In the same move, Rayburn hip-checked one twin before tail-swiping the other. When he took a bow, he stayed down long enough for the twins to smash into each other over his head.

They were on a roll! Winnie called every contact she had to get Rayburn more bouts. One day she got extra lucky. "Okay, so there're no spots left in the Super Smash Down," she said, putting her phone down. "But some lizard dude in the Eastern League is shedding his skin right now."

"Ew. Gross!" Rayburn said as he jogged on the treadmill.

Winnie wrinkled her nose. "Ugh, I know! So, they'll take us as a replacement. The only catch is this guy you're going to wrestle is really big."

"How big?" asked Rayburn.

"I mean huge! Enormous!" Winnie replied. "Think of the biggest thing you've ever seen!"

Turned out, Winnie had been underselling it. When they waited in their corner of the Eastern League ring, she watched in horror as Mr. Yokozuner stepped into the arena. The ground shook as he stomped his way toward the ring. Once inside, the giant sumo lizard, covered in red and black scales, towered over Rayburn. And to top it off, the monster was as wide as he was tall.

When the bout began, Mr. Yokozuner simply stood there as Rayburn tried to put any kind of wrestling hold on him. Rayburn looked as if he were trying to move a marble statue. Nothing budged on the humongous lizard.

"Oh, come on!" Rayburn shouted in frustration.

Finally, Mr. Yokozuner picked up Rayburn with one hand and easily hurled him across the ring. Rayburn slammed into the turnbuckle, and the giant lizard waddled after him. Rayburn tried to flee, but Mr. Yokozuner pushed into him, squishing his enormous belly into Rayburn. Soon he was swallowed completely by rolls of flab.

"Ugh!" Rayburn grunted. "It's in my mouth!"

Winnie gagged. "Ugh!"

You wouldn't know it to look at him, but

Rayburn and Winnie actually had a plan. The week before, Winnie had come up with a new dance move.

"The only way we're going to beat him is by getting him on his back," she had said back at the gym.

"So how do we do that?" Rayburn had asked, still running on the treadmill.

Winnie smiled. "We're going to need some help."

Winnie had had the brilliant idea to invite one of Rayburn's Pittsmore teammates to help him train.

Axehammer poked her head out from around the corner. "Long time no see, Steve," she said, batting her long eyelashes at him.

"What?" Rayburn asked. Surprised, he stumbled and fell face-first onto the treadmill. It shot him back, and he skidded across the gym floor.

Once he recovered, Winnie set the new training exercise in motion. She switched on some music and instructed Axehammer to run across the gym, at full speed, toward Rayburn. Then, just before she would slam into him . . .

"Now lift!" Winnie shouted.

Rayburn grabbed Axehammer around the waist and hoisted her into the air—a dance move they had seen in one of their favorite movies. Or, at least, he *tried* to lift her into the air. The heavy monster simply bowled him over before he got a chance.

"Do it again," Winnie ordered.

This time Rayburn caught Axehammer's waist and lifted her above his head . . . for about half a second. The heavy monster flopped down on top of him.

"And again," said Winnie.

Axehammer ran at Rayburn again and again. Rayburn lifted her again and again. Each time, he held her for a bit longer before she flattened him.

Rayburn grunted as he scrambled out from under the heavy monster. "This is my nightmare."

"Again!" Winnie ordered.

They'd drilled until Rayburn finally held Axehammer high above his head. She spread her arms and legs triumphantly as Rayburn slowly spun.

"That's it!" Winnie shouted. "You got it!"

Back at the match, Rayburn continued to get pounded by Mr. Yokozuner. The enormous lizard was expressionless as he flung Rayburn into a turnbuckle.

"Okay," Winnie shouted. "Get ready!"

Rayburn crouched and shook his head to clear it. "Nobody puts Ray-Ray in a corner."

The entire ring shook as Mr. Yokozuner thundered toward him. He seemed to move in slow motion as his massive frame jiggled closer and closer. The huge monster was almost on top of Rayburn, ready to slam him with massive tonnage.

"And now!" Winnie ordered. "Do the lift!"

Rayburn spread his arms wide, reaching as far around Mr. Yokozuner as possible. Then, using his opponent's momentum, Rayburn lifted with all his might. The sumo lizard's eyes widened as he rose off the mat. Rayburn raised him high over his head, slowly spinning. Mr. Yokozuner's stubby legs kicked as Rayburn heaved him over the ropes. The giant lizard flew through the air and landed outside the ring on his back. His arms and legs flailed, but he couldn't get up!

Winnie was thrilled as she circled Rayburn on her hoverbike. And even though he was completely exhausted, Rayburn seemed exhilarated too.

11
THE REAL TAKEDOWN

"Come on, McGinty, this isn't true monster wrestling," Marc Remy said, pounding the desk in frustration. "It's an affront to the sport and you know it. We all should be shocked and appalled."

"I have to disagree with you there, Marc," said Lights Out McGinty. The monster gave a wide grin. "They've won against several really tough opponents. And the way Steve combines traditional Cuban salsa with a hint of modern swing, then finishes with a lovely technical lift. That is a high degree of difficulty right there."

Winnie sat with Rayburn at the end of the long desk. She didn't like the way Marc Remy talked about their wrestling style, but she took a deep breath, trying to keep her cool. After all, this was their first live interview. What kind of coach would she look like if she pummeled the first reporter who gave her grief? Maybe she could save that for the fourth or fifth interview, once she was more established.

Marc Remy turned back to the camera. "Joining us now from their latest match is Winnie Coyle and Steve the Stupendous." He turned to Winnie and Rayburn. "Well, guys, congratulations on your latest win. But please, somebody admit it, this is hardly wrestling. You know that, right?"

"Yeah, but . . ." Winnie shrugged and smiled. "We're doing pretty well, aren't we?"

McGinty bobbed up and down with laughter. "She's got you there, Marc."

Marc rolled his eyes. "Whatever. You won a couple against some very, very questionable opponents. I'll give you that much. But what's next for Steve the Stupendous?"

"Well, he's feeling good," Winnie replied. "We're ready for our next match. And we want it to be back in Stoker!"

Both Marc and Lights Out were speechless.

"We'll wrestle any monster," Winnie continued. She turned to address the camera. "Coaches, give me a call!"

"Are you trying to tell me you think you're ready for a big match in Stoker?" asked Marc.

"Yes," Rayburn replied with a confident nod. "We are ready!"

Winnie and Rayburn made their way back to Stoker in the highest of spirits. Not only had they held their own in their first interview, but also King Gorge's coach had called Winnie right away. The bull-horned bulldog had agreed to wrestle Rayburn, or Steve the Stupendous actually, in the Jimbo Coyle Stadium, right there in Stoker. Even though she rode atop Rayburn's head, Winnie felt as if she were riding on a cloud. She was a real monster wrestling coach, with a real monster wrestling monster, ready to save the stadium. She had everything she had ever wanted.

The townspeople of Stoker seemed to be on board too. As they moved through town, many of the FOR LEASE signs had disappeared from business windows. Even Fred unfurled a banner over what was left of his Tentacular sign. Large bold letters spelled out: HOME OF STEVE THE STUPENDOUS.

"New sign is looking good, Fred," Winnie shouted down to him.

"Thanks, Winnie!" Fred replied with a wave. "I made it myself!"

"S-T-O-K-E-R!" spelled Winnie.

"Stoker!" Rayburn called back.

"S-T-E-V-E!" Winnie chanted.

"Steve!" replied Rayburn.

"Stoker Steve! Stoker Steve!" Winnie and Rayburn chanted together as they turned toward the stadium.

Winnie felt the spring in Rayburn's step as they went around back. She was excited too. She was so excited that she hardly noticed the flatbed trucks parked outside the gym entrance. However, after Rayburn gleefully kicked open the gym doors, she couldn't help but notice all the movers hauling away their training equipment. Dozens of workers carried out oversize weights, punching bags, and even the monster-sized footprints Winnie had made for Rayburn's footwork training.

Winnie slid down Rayburn's body. "What's going on?" she asked as she landed on the gym floor.

The town treasurer stepped forward, clipboard in hand. "I'm sorry, Winnie. I know all of this really old, completely useless stuff means a lot to you, but we have to clear it out. They need to rig this place to blow—"

"What!?" Winnie interrupted.

". . . up. And explode," the treasurer finished.

"No, no, no, no, they can't do that," Winnie pleaded. "We don't need to sell to Jimothy. We just got a match right here in Stoker!"

The treasurer shrugged. "Jimothy sweetened the deal if we moved up the signing date." She glanced at her clipboard. "And . . . it's a lot of money."

Winnie's stomach churned. All her big plans seemed to have been for nothing.

"Please," she pleaded. "There must be something you can do."

"I'm sorry. You're too late," the treasurer said, checking her watch. "The mayor is signing the deal at Slitherpoole Stadium this afternoon."

Winnie refused to give up. "Then it's not too late," she said. "We can make it!"

"You're never going to get there in time," said the treasurer. She shrugged and glanced up at Rayburn. "Unless you run really, really fast."

Rayburn smiled and lowered a hand to the ground. "Come on!"

Winnie hopped onto his outstretched palm and rode it like an elevator up to Rayburn's shoulder. Once she was in position, Rayburn dashed out of the gym and sprinted across the countryside.

Winnie knew Rayburn was running as fast as he could. She just hoped all of his hours on the treadmill would give him enough stamina to get there in time.

When they finally reached the Slitherpoole city limits, Rayburn poured on the speed, heading toward their stadium. Once inside, Winnie spotted a camera crew filming Tentacular in the middle of the huge ring. From the banners and bottles of sports drinks scattered about, it looked as if it was a commercial for his new drink: Tentaculade.

Winnie spotted the mayor of Stoker standing atop a turnbuckle next to Jimothy. Siggy floated on his hoverbike nearby.

"Wait! Stop!" she shouted. "We don't need to do this! Don't sign!"

Everyone in the stadium turned to see them run toward the ring. Rayburn quickly placed Winnie on the turnbuckle before leaning forward, gasping for breath.

The mayor held up the contract. "I already did...."

Ignoring Winnie, Jimothy snatched the papers from the mayor's hands. He pulled out a pen and spun the mayor around, using his back as a table.

"Hold on!" Winnie shouted.

"What?" Jimothy asked, annoyed.

"Mr. Jimothy! Stoker has a new champion wrestler that everyone in Stoker is going to come see," Winnie explained. "So we don't need your money!"

"Is that true, Winnie?" asked the mayor.

"Yes!" she replied, pointing at Rayburn. Although, she wished he had already caught his breath and still wasn't doubled over. "Steve over here just got a bigtime match in Stoker against King Gorge!"

"That's...right," Rayburn added between wheezes.

"King Gorge?" asked Tentacular. He laughed in a booming voice. "Oh man, he hasn't come out of his kennel since I destroyed him. He's broken. Everybody in the game knows that."

"I mean, I heard his coach was desperate,"

Jimothy added, jutting a thumb at Winnie and Rayburn. "But these guys?"

"Yeah, pretty tragic," Tentacular agreed. "Sign the papers, Jimothy."

"I . . . I don't understand," said Winnie.

"Oh, you don't get it, do you?" Tentacular asked. "It was never about the money." He pointed at himself with one of his tentacles. "Stoker Stadium is coming down because *I* want it to."

Winnie shook her head in confusion. "But . . . why?"

"Because no matter how many championships I win, some chump's always going to tell me that I'm not as good as Rayburn," Tentacular replied. "So I figure, I can live in his shadow, or I can tear down everything that casts that shadow."

"Wow, and I thought I had issues," Rayburn Junior said, finally catching his breath. "That's just crazy. . . ."

With lightning speed, Tentacular reached out of the ring and wrapped his tentacles around Rayburn's neck. "Who asked you!?" Rayburn choked and squirmed as Tentacular lifted him off the ground. He pulled him close to his face. "You make me sick. Monsters wrestle. Sometimes they destroy cities, but they definitely . . . don't . . . dance!"

"Hey, put him down!" Winnie ordered.

"Okay," Tentacular said with a smile. He flung Rayburn across the stadium to smash into a row of seats.

"Please don't do this," Winnie pleaded. "That stadium is everything to that town. To me. Please don't take that away."

"Winnie, this isn't about you. It's all about *me*." Tentacular nodded toward his manager. "Sign the papers, Jimothy."

Winnie watched helplessly as the papers were signed and the stadium's fate was sealed. Her lips trembled as she rounded on Siggy. "You're okay with this? With him destroying everything you and my dad built?"

"Let me tell you something," Siggy said. "I loved your dad. He did great things with Rayburn. But now it's my chance to do great things with Tentacular. That's wrestling." He flew his bike closer and shook his head. "What you're doing . . . I'm just glad Jimbo isn't around to see it."

Winnie slumped and lowered her head, defeated.

Rayburn helped her off the turnbuckle and they left the stadium. Rayburn shuffled to a nearby playground and set her down beside a bench. While she plopped down, Rayburn sat on a nearby set of monkey bars. The dome-shaped structure bent and sank under his weight.

Winnie wiped tears from her eyes. For some crazy reason, she had believed a sixteen-year-old girl could be a real monster wrestling coach. Maybe Siggy was right. Maybe her father would be ashamed of her coaching style. She had taken the son of a championship wrestler and turned him into the joke of the WMW. Rayburn deserved so much better than her.

"You have enough money to pay back Lady Mayhen now," Winnie told him. "You don't need me. Just leave me alone."

"Even if I wanted to, I'm pretty sure I . . . live here now," Rayburn joked, glancing down at the crushed monkey bars wrapped around his bottom.

"I thought I was saving the stadium," Winnie said, wiping her eyes. "But really I was playing at being a coach. And I couldn't even do that right."

"Hey, come on," Rayburn said. "We got knocked down, so we get back up."

"No, not this time," Winnie said. She remembered what Rayburn had told her when they first met. "I'm staying down."

She got to her feet and started the long walk back to Stoker.

"Just so you know, I'm not agreeing with you," Rayburn said. His grunts joined the sounds of twisting metal. "I'm actually really stuck."

12
NO MORE LOSING

That night, Rayburn returned to the only life he had ever known. He made his way back to Pittsmore and the underground fight club. He sighed as he entered the old warehouse, shuffling through the familiar sounds and smells of another fight night gearing up.

Denise was the first monster to spot him. She rolled up to him as he headed for the locker room. "Well, well, look who's back," she said with a wide grin.

Rayburn didn't reply. He simply handed her a suitcase full of money. His debt to Lady Mayhen was paid in full from all his winnings. Now he could go back to losing.

Rayburn thought he would feel relieved coming back to Pittsmore. No more getting up early. No more special diet. No more weight training. No more treadmill. Now he could go back to easy living. Just go out there, lose his matches, come back and do his favorite thing—nothing. But he didn't feel relieved at all. Overall, he felt pretty rotten.

As Rayburn opened his locker, an enormous shadow fell over him.

"Welcome back, twinkle toes," said Lady Mayhen. "We missed you!" She gestured to the crowd outside. "It seems like you are the hot new favorite after all your adventures." She aimed a long red talon at him. "There is a lot of money on you to win tonight. So you go in that ring . . . and lose." She smiled and pinched his cheek. "You were always my best loser."

Rayburn's shoulders sank as she tromped away. As he dug through his locker for a towel, something ached in the pit of his stomach. He had never had stage fright or pre-match butterflies before. It had to be something else. Was it something he ate?

Rayburn's eyes widened when he realized what it was. The thought of losing literally made him sick to his stomach. It didn't matter that he had danced his way to victory so many times. The thought of returning to a life of losing made him physically ill.

Rayburn shook his head. He'd have to get over that quick. What else was he supposed to do?

As he fumbled through his locker, his claws came across a thin strip of paper. He pulled out an old photo strip from a monster photo booth. The images showed his dad and him posing for each shot. His father flexed his giant muscles while a much younger Rayburn Junior tried to mimic his dad's moves.

Rayburn smiled. He had always worried about growing up in the shadow of his father, the greatest wrestler of all time. But now, thanks to Winnie, Rayburn had become his own wrestler, with his own style. Thanks to her, he didn't feel intimidated by his father anymore. He wished he could've helped her the same way she had helped him.

Then, while staring at the father and son photos, Rayburn thought he had an idea to do just that.

Rayburn slammed the locker shut and left the club. He ran all night, making his way back to Stoker. When he got there, he noticed that the entire town was gathered in front of the stadium. Tentacular and Jimothy were there, as well as a few news crews. Unfortunately, he didn't see Winnie anywhere in the crowd. Rayburn ran to her house and peeked into her second-story window.

"Ahh!" Winnie shouted, startled by the giant eyeball staring at her. "What are you doing here?"

"Sorry, I should've called first," Rayburn replied. "But you know, I don't have a phone . . . or pockets." He smiled. "Look, I need my coach back."

Winnie shook her head. "Don't you get it? We're a total joke. We don't belong in the ring."

"Hey, you know that feeling that you have right now?" Rayburn asked. "That's how I've felt my whole life. I spent so much time running away from what I thought I *should* be that I never found out what I *could* be."

Winnie shook her head again, confused.

"And now I have!" Rayburn continued. "I know that I'm never going to be the greatest wrestler of all time, or win the Big Belt, and that is just fine. But I am *not* going back to being a loser." He pointed at her. "And that's on you. You ruined losing for me. And you know what? It feels good! I feel good for the first time. So, thank you."

"Rayburn . . . I . . . ," Winnie began. Then she leaped out the window and latched onto his neck, giving the monster a monster of a hug. "Thank you!"

"Okay, okay." Rayburn plucked Winnie from his neck and placed her in his palm. "Enough with the sappy stuff. I'm here to help you save that stadium."

"What?" Winnie stepped back, shaking her head. "No. It's too late. We could fill it a thousand times and Tentacular would still blow it up."

"Yeah?" Rayburn smiled. "We'll see about that."

13
TRASH TALK

Winnie actually felt hopeful after Rayburn filled her in on his plan. Tentacular was so arrogant that he just might fall for it. She also told Rayburn a little secret about the champ that might put them over the top. They had to work quickly though, so they had discussed everything while sneaking into the back of the stadium.

Once they were sure that they had disconnected all the explosives, they made their way to the main entrance. The *boo*s from the Stoker townspeople grew louder as they neared the statue of Jimbo Coyle. Winnie and Rayburn peeked around the statue to see people actually pelting Jimbo and Tentacular with garbage.

"Hey, buddy," Jimothy told Tentacular. "I'm getting hurt here, so if we can blow this thing up and go, that would be great."

"With pleasure," Tentacular said as he scooped up a detonator with his tentacles. He raised the plunger and grinned widely.

"Five, four, three, two, one," counted Jimothy. "Go!"

Tentacular pushed the plunger, but nothing happened.

Jimothy blinked in surprise. "Well, that was disappointing."

Winnie rode on Rayburn's shoulder as he stepped out from behind the statue. "What's the matter, boys?" he asked. "You show up, but no blow up? Hey, that rhymes!"

Tentacular threw up his tentacles in frustration. "Oh, not these clowns again."

"That's right!" said Winnie.

"What? Are you scared of clowns?" asked Rayburn. "I mean, obviously some of them seem kind of creepy, but you know . . . us?"

"Yeah! And we're here to challenge you, champ," Winnie added. "Or should I say, *chump*?"

Tentacular scowled. "Wait, chump?"

"You heard her," Rayburn said. "I'm calling you out, *spent*-tacular! I'm going to wrestle you. Right here in Stoker."

Tentacular roared with laughter. "Yeah right. Now, why would I wrestle a nobody loser like you, Steve?"

Rayburn confidently stepped forward. "Because my name's not Steve. I'm the son of the greatest monster wrestler of all time." He put his hands on his hips. "My name is Rayburn Junior."

Gasps, murmurs, and camera flashes rippled through the crowd.

Tentacular's eyes widened. "You're Rayburn's kid?"

"You bet he is," Winnie replied. "And you can blow up all the stadiums you want, but you'll always be in the shadow of the real greatest wrestler of all time . . . Rayburn."

The gathered townspeople cheered. Then they began to chant. "Rayburn! Rayburn! Rayburn!"

"You want to prove you're the greatest?" Winnie asked him. "Then fight the greatest name in monster wrestling!"

Tentacular stomped forward. He loomed over Rayburn, face-to-face. "I would destroy you."

"Oh, like you destroyed King Gorge?" Winnie asked. "Why don't you *tell* us all about that one?"

"What are you talking about?" Tentacular asked. Rayburn licked his nose, the same way King Gorge had done. Tentacular reared back as if he had been stung. "Oh, no, no, no!"

"What was it, the third round?" Winnie asked. "I bet we could beat that, Rayburn?"

"We said one, not three," Rayburn whispered to her. "We were going to go for *one* round."

"I got excited," Winnie whispered back. "Just go with it."

Rayburn cleared his throat. "Right! Three. That's right."

The champ laughed. "You think you could go three rounds with Tentacular?"

"Ohhh, I think we should make a bet," Winnie said, loud enough for everyone to hear.

"A bet!?" asked Tentacular.

"We'll go three rounds with you . . . ," Winnie began.

"And if I survive, Stoker keeps the stadium,"

Rayburn finished. "I mean . . . unless you're scared."

Tentacular snarled at them before glancing back at the crowd. The townspeople, the news crews, everyone was waiting for his reply. He finally threw up his tentacles in disgust.

"Fine!" he roared. "It's on!" He leaned in and poked a tentacle into Rayburn's chest. "By the time Tentacular's done, there's not going to be a thing left of you, this town, or your overrated dads." He turned to the crowd and spread his tentacles wide. "Tentacular's going to bury it all!"

"Let's see you try!" Winnie shouted. "Let's see you try right here in Stoker!"

"Rayburn! Rayburn! Rayburn!" chanted the townspeople. "Stoker! Stoker! Stoker!"

Tentacular trembled with rage. Before storming away, he balled his tentacles into a fist and backhanded the statue of Jimbo Coyle. The statue tumbled over the city before landing on a hill on the other side of town.

14
GAUNTLET OF DOOM

Back in his Pittsmore days, Rayburn occasionally had a Steve the Stupendous fan or two. They never lasted long, of course. There were only so many times you could watch the same monster lose before you decided to root for another one. Needless to say, Rayburn was totally unprepared to have an entire town full of fans. And they weren't Steve fans; they were truly his fans—Rayburn Junior fans.

Now, any monster can *say* that he or she is the hometown hero with an entire city full of fans. But the town of Stoker proved it when each and every one of them came out to support him and help him train for his three-round bout against Tentacular.

Trucks rolled to the outskirts of town, each

loaded with all kinds of construction equipment—metal panels, loads of logs, and rolls and rolls of hoses. Once there, they spent the better part of a day assembling the perfect training tool.

Rayburn was awestruck when Winnie showed him the finished product. A monster-size obstacle course spanned the countryside. Giant barricades, skeletal steel structures, and huge pieces of construction machinery stood between him and the finish line. He smiled as he thought of everyone's dedication to helping him win.

"The town has come together and built this spectacular, anti-Tentacular agility and evasion training device," she explained as she came about on her hoverbike. "Otherwise known as . . . the Gauntlet of Doom!"

Rayburn's smile vanished. "That's not a fun name."

Winnie nodded at him. "If you can get through this, you might just last three rounds with Tentacular."

As Rayburn moved to the starting line, the townspeople gathered behind him. Fred unfolded a lawn chair and plopped down. "Free side of waffle fries if you win, Rayburn," he said. "With purchase of a large sandwich, of course."

"You're too kind," Rayburn replied.

Rayburn leaned forward, ready to start. He gazed down at the hodgepodge of metal structures and construction equipment. It didn't look so hard.

Winnie pressed a button on her phone and the Gauntlet of Doom earned its name. Flames erupted from behind obstacles, spikes jutted out of structures, and masses of fire hoses, mimicking tentacles, flailed from behind barriers.

Rayburn swallowed hard. "Uh-oh."

"You can do this," Winnie told him.

Rayburn yelled a battle cry as he charged into the gauntlet. Unfortunately, the first set of hoses encircled him and flung him off to the side. That was the first time Rayburn had heard an entire town groan in disappointment. He stumbled back to the starting line, ready to try again.

Winnie hovered close. "We're going to use every trick you learned in the underground," she said. "Every step you learned on your global dance journey."

Rayburn took off again, more determined than ever.

"Every fake out and fox-trot," Winnie continued.

"Singing in the Rain! The Worm! Keep dancing!"

As she called out dances, Rayburn used them against the obstacles. He backed into a box step to avoid the hoses. He swung around a crane arm to avoid a wrecking ball. And he rhythmically writhed on his belly, ducking blasts of flames.

"They say offense is the best defense," Winnie said as she zoomed along beside him. "No! *Defense* is the best defense!"

Rayburn grabbed another set of flailing hoses and tied them into a knot.

"It doesn't have to look pretty," Winnie continued. "It just has to get us through the third."

"Come on!" Rayburn said as he moonwalked away from a set of snapping metal jaws. "This looks pretty!"

The dancing monster tapped, samba'd, waltzed, and limbo'd his way through the course. Depending on the obstacle, he easily leaped, dipped, fossied, or sidestepped his way clear of any danger. And what obstacles he couldn't dodge, he wrecked and smashed. His brute strength had grown along with his fancy footwork. He was doing it! Maybe he stood a chance against Tentacular after all.

Rayburn leaned forward as he charged toward a poster of Tentacular plastered across a barricade. "To victory!" he shouted, before crashing through. He skidded to a stop on the other side when he saw four familiar monster faces. Klonk, Axehammer, Denise, and Nerdle were waiting for him. "Surprise!" they shouted, Nerdle giving an energetic wave.

"Hey!" Rayburn said, catching his breath. "What's up, you guys?"

Winnie pulled up on her hoverbike. "Congrats! You're halfway there!"

Rayburn stumbled in surprise. "Halfway!?"

"My dad's statue is the finish line," Winnie said, pointing to a distant bronze figure on the hill. It was so far away, Rayburn could barely see what it was.

"That's not fair!" he protested.

"You're not in a fair fight," Winnie replied, moving her hoverbike toward him. "Tentacular is bigger, faster, stronger, and better looking than you. If he does catch you, you need to get away, and fast. Let's see what you got!"

Rayburn noticed the Pittsmore monsters closing in. A couple swung steel girders as weapons as they surrounded him. He didn't like the look of this.

"Get him!" Winnie ordered.

The monsters roared as they charged. But instead of running, Rayburn flash-danced toward them. He rolled over Klonk's back, whipping his tail overhead to bat away Denise like a soccer ball. She smacked into Nerdle, knocking him down like a bowling pin.

As Rayburn charged toward Axehammer, she raised her arms, preparing to be lifted. Rayburn faked her out by leaping over her, his arms jutting out in a graceful swan dive. Unfortunately, the landing wasn't as graceful. He smashed into the ground, his own face breaking his fall.

A terrifying roar sounded behind him. Rayburn turned to discover that it had come from Denise. She roared again, opening her mouth unnaturally wide, baring rows and rows of razor-sharp teeth.

"Get him, Denise!" Axehammer shouted.

The monsters cheered as the ferocious fur ball rolled toward him, her mouth snapping open and shut. Rayburn didn't have a special dance move for this situation. He simply ran. It was all about stamina at this point as he kept just ahead of Denise's sharp teeth.

Luckily, it wasn't long before Denise ran out of steam and started to fall back. Rayburn was about to take a breather himself when Winnie appeared, driving a huge tractor with a wicked claw at the end of a long arm.

"Heads up!" Winnie shouted as the arm batted Denise out of the way. "Sorry!"

Rayburn poured on the speed as the giant machine closed in. Denise's biting mouth was replaced by the biting jaws of the tractor's grabber. He barely kept his tail from being snagged in its claw.

Winnie laughed as she aimed the tractor at him. "You're not done yet!"

They went up and down hills and zigzagged over field after field. Winnie finally let up when Rayburn reached the statue. Panting heavily and utterly exhausted, Rayburn stumbled toward the statue and placed a finger on Jimbo's shiny foot.

"Am I ready now?" he asked before collapsing in a heap.

Winnie climbed down from the tractor and onto Rayburn's arm. She kicked back, placing her hands behind her head. "You're ready."

15
THE COACH SPEECH

The last time Winnie had been inside a packed Jimbo Coyle Stadium was one of the most disappointing times of her life. Stoker had lost its monster wrestler one moment and the stadium itself the next. But now Stoker had a new monster, a better one, as far as she was concerned, and they actually had a chance to save the stadium. This time she wouldn't be a mere spectator, simply watching the action. She was a real WMW coach who would be right in the thick of things. Her heart pounded with excitement. Even though she and Rayburn were deep under the stadium in the locker room, the droning buzz from the crowd above was electrifying.

Rayburn shadowboxed nearby to warm up. Winnie wondered if he was as nervous as she was. She moved her hoverbike closer to him.

"Okay, Ray," she said. "I'm not going to give you the coach speech, because I'm terrible at them."

Rayburn stopped boxing and smiled. "Well, I don't know if I'd say you're . . ." He nodded and shrugged. "Okay, yeah, you are."

"Funny," Winnie said with a laugh. Then her smile faded as she turned her hoverbike toward the door. "Let's go get our stadium back."

Rayburn nodded and marched out of the locker room. Winnie hovered beside him. The rumbling of the crowd grew louder, and spotlights washed over the end of the tunnel. As they neared the light, the rhythmic chanting became clear.

"Stoker! Stoker! Stoker! Stoker! Stoker!" said the crowd.

Rayburn and Winnie paused just inside the exit. Already, the sounds were almost deafening.

"Ladies and gentlemen . . . ," boomed the announcer's voice. "World Monster Wrestling presents . . . a special event! One stadium, one last chance, two monsters . . . The Smackdown to

Save the Stadium! In this corner, weighing in at twenty-two tons. Standing forty-three feet tall. From Stoker . . . Rayburn Junior!"

Upon hearing his name, Rayburn slid into the arena in a classic dance entrance. Music boomed through the speakers, and spotlights washed over him as the giant monster danced his way toward the ring.

The audience changed their chant. "Rayburn! Rayburn! Rayburn!"

Winnie followed the dancing monster on her hoverbike. As she neared the ring, she spotted Marc Remy and Lights Out McGinty in their usual commentator spots at ringside. The giant video screens above the ring alternated between Rayburn's dance and the two commentators.

"Oh yeah! I'm stoked to be back in Stoker!" Marc said.

"We all are!" agreed McGinty. "Tonight is going to go down in history as the greatest match ever, or the shortest, most painful embarrassment to ever happen in professional monster wrestling."

"Here we go, McGinty," said Remy. "Stoker's salsa sensation is making his way into the ring. And this crowd is just eating it up."

"You got this, Winnie!" someone shouted from the audience. Winnie turned and spotted Fred nudging the spectators around him. "Hey, everybody! I know her! She eats at my diner!"

Rayburn tried to climb through the ropes to get into the ring. Unfortunately, he tripped over the bottom one and spun around the others, becoming tangled. Like rubber bands, the ropes spun him back into the opposite direction and he flew out of them. He performed a summersault in midair and landed in the center of the ring. The audience cheered, thinking it was all part of his routine.

"Look at the confidence, Marc," Lights Out McGinty continued. "If he's scared, he is clearly not showing it."

"Somebody's got to say this about Rayburn Junior," said Marc Remy. "We know he's audacious, he's courageous, but three rounds with Tentacular? What the heck is he thinking!? He might've lost his monster mind. I just don't know."

"Let's not forget to mention that in his corner is the young rookie coach Winnie Coyle," McGinty added. "That's right, daughter of the legendary coach Jimbo Coyle."

Winnie tried to tune out the commentators. She pulled up to the turnbuckle and hopped off her hoverbike. Her mother was already there waiting for her. She smiled and placed both hands on Winnie's shoulders.

"No matter what happens tonight," her mom said, "I want you to remember, this stadium isn't your dad's legacy—you are."

Winnie smiled and gave her mom a hug. "Thanks, Mom."

Suddenly the lights snapped off and the audience fell silent.

"And now . . . ," boomed the announcer's voice. "In his return to Stoker, the undefeated reigning holder of the Big Belt . . . Tennnnnn-tacular!"

Music blasted from the speakers as Tentacular's bioluminescence exploded from the end of his entrance tunnel. His luminous body cycled through a few bodybuilding poses before the lights came up amid a barrage of *boo*s. The champ wore the championship belt around his waist and didn't seem to care what the audience thought.

"What's going on, Stoker?" Tentacular asked as he strutted toward the ring. Siggy rode his hoverbike behind him. The giant monster raised a tentacle to the side of his head as if waiting for a reply. Then he removed the belt and raised it high over his head. "Oh, you miss this? Forget about it! Because you ain't ever seeing one of these again!"

Winnie watched Rayburn stare at Tentacular before he glanced up at the banners hanging over the ring. Jimbo and Rayburn Senior seemed to be staring back at him.

"Ray?" Winnie asked. "You okay?"

The monster didn't respond.

"Rayburn!" Winnie shouted. "Look at me! Are you with me?"

Rayburn turned to her, and she no longer saw that confident monster that danced his way into the ring. Instead, she saw the eyes of little Ray-Ray, her childhood friend. He suddenly seemed unsure and out of place.

"Hey, I get it," Winnie said, pointing up at the banners. "Their story was heroic and awesome and super serious. And ours is . . ." She shrugged. "Ours is a dumb comedy. But you know what? I love dumb comedies!"

Rayburn's face softened. "Me too!"

"Especially ones about friends," she added.

The big monster leaned forward and smiled, his eyes shining brightly. That was the Rayburn she wanted to see.

Winnie put her hands on her hips. "So, are you ready to look stupid?"

"Yes!" Rayburn replied.

"How stupid!?" she asked.

Rayburn laughed. "Really, really stupid!"

"And do we care?" Winnie asked.

Rayburn shook his head. "We don't care!"

Winnie cupped a hand behind her ear. "Uh, I can't hear you!"

"We! Do! Not! Care!" Rayburn yelled, punching the air with each word.

"Now, buck up," Winnie ordered. "Put on your game face, because it's time to wrestle! And dance! Both!"

"Whoa, whoa, time out!" Rayburn's eyes widened as he leaned closer. "You just did the coach speech."

Winnie shook her head. "Wait, I did, didn't I?"

A grin stretched across Rayburn's face. "And it was great!"

"It was?" she asked.

"Yeah. I mean, you know . . ." He shrugged. "It was a little weird. But it was great!"

Winnie couldn't believe it. She had successfully given the big coach speech. And not only that, but the fact that she stood in the center of her father's stadium, surrounded by cheering fans . . . she finally felt like a real monster wrestling coach.

The referee flew into the ring on his hoverbike. "All right, wrestlers!" he shouted. "To the center of the ring."

Winnie nodded at Rayburn. "Okay, let's go make it through the third," she said. "And if you live, let's get frozen yogurt after!"

Rayburn beamed. "I love frozen yogurt!" Then his grin vanished. "Wait . . . if I live!?"

Winnie chuckled and shooed him out of the corner. She watched proudly as Rayburn joined Tentacular and the referee in the center of the ring.

Her mom had told her that *she* was her father's legacy, not some old stadium. As Winnie watched her monster stand toe-to-toe against a champion monster wrestler, she was beginning to believe it. And she knew she wasn't the only one. Rayburn was his father's legacy too. They had learned so much and had come so far. Winnie nodded and smiled. No matter what anyone said, she knew that both of their fathers would be proud.

Win or lose, they were a true monster wrestling team!